The Case Files of Henri Davenforth

Case File 8

Honor Raconteur

This Potion is DA BOMB

Published by Raconteur House
Plymouth, MI

THIS POTION IS DA BOMB
The Case Files of Henri Davenforth Case 8

A Raconteur House book/ published by arrangement with the author

Copyright © 2022 by Honor Raconteur
Cover by Katie Griffin
*Orange or grapefruit juice explosion in slow motion.*by Relight Motion/Shutterstock; *Firey Exploding Burst* by ArenaCreative/Depositphotos; *Clockwork spare parts* by donatas1205/Shutterstock; *male man toilet WC* by yougifted/Shutterstock; *vintage bronze seamless background* by Kompaniets Taras/Shutterstock

This book is a work of fiction, so please treat it like a work of fiction. Seriously. References to real people, dead people, good guys, bad guys, stupid politicians, companies, restaurants, cats with attitudes, events, products, dragons, locations, pop culture references, or wacky historical events are intended to provide a sense of authenticity and are used fictitiously. Or because I wanted it in the story. Characters, names, story, location, dialogue, weird humor and strange incidents all come from the author's very fertile imagination and are not to be construed as real. No, I don't believe in killing off main characters. Villains are a totally different story.

All rights reserved.

No part of this book may be reproduced, scanned, or distributed in any printed or electronic form without permission. Please do not participate in or encourage electronic piracy of copyrighted materials in violation of the author's rights. NO AI/NO BOT. We do not consent to any Artificial Intelligence (AI), generative AI, large language model, machine learning, chatbot, or other automated analysis, generative process, or replication program to reproduce, mimic, remix, summarize, or otherwise replicate any part of this creative work, via any means: print, graphic, sculpture, multimedia, audio, or other medium. We support the right of humans to control their artistic works. (All typos are left on purpose to prove it's not AI written.)

For information address: www.raconteurhouse.com

Report 01: Children are Not to be Trusted

I entered my office on palace grounds with a box in my hands. My new office was attached to Jamie's new division, the Queen's Own, for eminently practical reasons. First, I needed to be close in order to assist her. Second, it was the only office that had room for me. The building housing the other royal mages was full up until someone retired. Which, at their ages, wouldn't happen any time soon.

I didn't mind the location at all. The office was on the larger side—certainly larger than my old office at the precinct—with windows overlooking the grounds. I'd been filling it with things the past few days. Most of my reference books were here, and I had two large chalkboards hanging on one wall, potion ingredients and tools dominating another on orderly shelves. I was bringing in little things now. Like more empty journals, as mine were dangerously full and in evidence lockup.

A knock sounded on my open door before Jamie strode in. She had a portfolio in hand, a smile on her face. I'd yet to see her this morning, and it was always a delight when she came to me.

"Good morning, my darling," she caroled as she entered, kissing me chastely.

Oh, she was in a good mood this morning. "Good morning. To what do I owe the pleasure?"

"First, have lunch with all of us. We're doing a meet and greet with our new hires."

I perked up slightly. "Oh, did you find some, then?"

"I did. Well, Gibs did. He's found us a librarian to run the evidence lockup and archives—"

Now there was a perfect choice. No one catalogued or organized better than a librarian.

"—and a retired teacher to run the front desk. I figure, anyone who can handle unruly kids can handle the crazy people."

"Truly." I nodded in approval. These sounded like excellent candidates. "I'll need to train the librarian on how to handle the magical evidence."

"You will," she agreed readily. "You and Colette, anyway. I know you've been working on a manual for that."

"More like I've been revising the police manual. It's mostly up to date now, but Colette is looking it over to see if I've missed anything."

"Cool beans. While I have you, I want a second opinion." Jamie flipped open the portfolio and showed me the top illustration. "We've been given two choices on our new uniforms."

It had been decided by Queen Regina that this new branch of the kingsmen needed its own uniform. She wanted the people at large to understand that this division was over investigations—their own task force as it were. New uniforms would be a physical representation of that. I quite liked the idea of not wearing red on red.

The top illustration showed a woman in full uniform. The woman looked rather like Jamie, so I had a good idea whom the artist had used as a model. At first glance, I heartily approved of the design. This uniform consisted of black pants, a black coat, with a red vest and white shirt. The coat had pockets and collar, and red piping along the sleeves, giving it a sharp look.

"Second choice." Jamie flipped the page over to reveal what was underneath.

The second choice was interesting. No red piping

on the coat, same vest, but the pants were distinctly different. They were tapered in the leg, with pockets just above the knee on both sides.

I pointed at it. "I must say, I like the look of that. Those large pockets will come in handy."

"Right? They're called cargo pants in my world. Although they're typically wide in the leg, not tapered, but anyway. Pocket space is handy. I suggested it to the designer and he really liked the idea. So far, everyone's voted option two."

"I do as well." I glanced down at my own legs. "Although can I request my pants not be tapered?"

"Now, Henri." Jamie waggled her eyebrows in that teasing manner she had. "Your legs are sexy."

I gave her a droll look. Why did she like to tease me so much? "There is nothing sexy about my legs. Not that you would know—you've never seen them."

"I have too. That time when we had evidence in the lake and you had to ditch your boots and roll up your cuffs to wade in, remember?"

Oh. Actually, I had momentarily forgotten that.

I was saved from an actual response when my pad rang. With no little relief, I answered it with alacrity. Why was my sister calling? I'd just seen her a half hour ago. "Emilia, what is it?"

"*My dear brother,*" she drawled, sounding on the verge of laughter, "*you have been pickpocketed.*"

I blinked down at the pad, quite sure I'd heard that wrong. "I beg your pardon?"

"*You heard me correctly. You've been pickpocketed. I have your wallet.*"

It wasn't that I didn't believe her; my sister has never lied to me in our lives. Still, my hand automatically went to my back pocket, where my wallet normally resided, needing to physically check. I felt nothing there, no bulge. Oh no.

"How do you have it?"

"*I caught your nephew throwing money over his head and giggling. I don't know how, but when you hugged him goodbye, the little scamp grabbed your wallet and took off with it. I just found it lying next to him.*"

Jamie doubled over laughing. "Pickpocketed by a one-year-old! Some policeman you are!"

I gave the love of my life a withering glare. "I'd like to point out that his own mother didn't notice he had it for the past half hour until he started throwing my money around. Great magic, where did he even learn how to do that?"

"*I have no idea. He likes to play with his father's wallet, maybe he's branching out now.*"

Jamie was still laughing, smile threatening to split her face. "He'll be a mob boss at age five at this rate."

Clearly, I could expect no help from that quarter. "Emilia, I'm not sure when I can get over there to retrieve it."

"*Actually, I need to do some errands. Can I just bring it to you? I haven't seen your new office yet. I'd love to do so.*"

"Oh, certainly. That'll be easier on me. Just message me when you're at the gate, I'll come get you."

"*Expect me in the next hour, then.*" She blew a kiss and rang off.

I didn't need to ask this question of my lover—I knew the answer. I asked it anyway. "You're never going to let me live this down, are you?"

"Never, ever," Jamie assured me brightly.

"You're going to tell the story to Seaton, too."

"At the very least."

As expected. "What bribe might I offer to ensure your silence?"

She leaned in and kissed me on the cheek. "There's not enough chocolate in the world for that. Sorry, love. Alright, I'm off to order the uniforms."

I groaned from the depths of my soul. Why did she

like telling stories so much?

"You're sunk now, Doctor."

I whirled to find Eddy Jameson, the little scamp, lounging in my windowsill for all the world like it was a chair and he'd popped 'round for tea. He'd grown over the past year and a half—there was more height to him—but he was still all elbows and knees with that irrepressible smile.

"Jameson! Kindly make noise when you walk before you give me heart failure."

His grin widened, kissing his ears. "Sounds less fun."

I growled at him wordlessly. He didn't seem at all intimidated.

Jamie had elected to take Jameson on as an apprentice. She'd said something about him being a grasshopper to her Jedi self, whatever that meant. In essence, she found his skills and talent too good to pass up, so he'd been brought into the Queen's Own as an apprentice spy. I'd been dubious about this because the boy had broken into the palace wards just to read books. His impulsive nature was sure to get him into trouble. He'd slowly mellowed, though, over the past year. I think it was Jamie's steadying influence.

"What are you here for?" I inquired, already resigned to his presence.

He blinked ingenuous brown eyes at me. "Can I borrow a book?"

Ah, of course. The usual with him, then. Jameson could read a book faster than any speed reader in the kingdom. I would bet my life's earnings on this. "Which one, or do you care?"

"Jamie said you had books written of the past cases you've worked with her."

I quirked a brow at him, questioning this interest. "You want to read about past cases? Surely that would be dry reading for you."

"No, no, I want to know how investigations go," he corrected hastily, hopping lightly down to the floor. "And Jamie investigates a case like no one else, right? It's why she's constantly training people."

I couldn't fault his logic. He was entirely correct. I did feel of two minds about letting him read them, as some parts of them were rather...private? Not quite the word I wanted, but something of that sentiment. On the other hand, the only time Jameson was well behaved was when he had a thick stack of books to be engrossed in.

Somewhat against my better judgement, I acquiesced. "Fine. Under two conditions. First, you must understand there's only one copy of these. I want you to read them in these offices. They are not to leave the building under any circumstances. Understood?"

He lit up with delight and placed a hand over his heart in a vow. "Promise. What's the second?"

"There's many a thing involved in those books that are not common knowledge. Before you handle them, I need to check how Jamie feels about this first."

His eyes shone with new excitement. "Trade secrets?"

"That is the very least of it." I answered absently, already writing a message to my lover. *Jamie, Jameson wants to read the case files.*

Her response was immediate. *And you're going to let him?*

If you're alright with it. It does mean him learning of your background.

Eh, he's already figured out half of it anyway. It's fine to tell him.

I had thought she wouldn't be upset about the possibility. She considered Jameson one of her own by now. I put the pad aside and regarded him thoughtfully. I best warn him of more than just her origins. "Jameson, listen carefully. This isn't information to noise about. Jamie's given her permission for me to tell you. Alright?"

He sobered, focus intent on me. "I won't betray her trust. Her, of all people, I'd never betray."

"I believe that. Very well, two warnings before you pick up those books. First of which is that Jamie isn't from this world."

His eyes went wide in his narrow face, mouth dropping slightly. "Blimey, really?"

"Truly. When Belladonna was at her peak of power and madness, she portaled people in from random worlds. Jamie is one of them."

I let him sit with this knowledge for a moment. Jameson, for all that I despaired of him, was incredibly intelligent. He could absorb facts quickly. It was both his downfall and his saving grace.

"It's why she knows so many things that are different," Jameson murmured, mostly to himself. "That's why."

"Yes. She brings knowledge from an entirely different world. We capitalize on that as much as possible. Much of what you will read in these accounts reference her world."

Jameson sat on it for another moment, still thinking, then inhaled a deep breath. "I'll keep the secret."

I inclined my head, pleased my instincts weren't wrong. "If I didn't think you could, and if Jamie didn't trust you, we wouldn't be having this conversation. You may talk about what you read, but only amongst a select few: myself, Gibson, Marshall, Evans, Bennett, Seaton, and Jamie herself. Do limit your questions to one of us."

His head bobbed in fervent agreement. "Absolutely. Promise."

"Very well. Second warning: The first book outlines how Jamie killed Belladonna."

His eyes popped wide again. "Cor!"

"Yes, quite. There's many a person who would love to read a firsthand account, but this is something else she doesn't talk about readily. Understand?"

He nodded and I saw sincerity in his expression. I still wasn't sure what to make of this curiosity, but Jamie had given her permission. I trusted Jameson's mouth to stay shut about what he read. I had no doubt about that. I went to my office safe, where I stored the volumes, and fetched the first one before handing it over.

Jameson took it with both hands, his face glowing with that light of anticipation whenever he was handed some rare book. He immediately squirreled himself into my wing-back chair in the corner, legs tucked up against his chest, and turned to the first page. Such was his focus, I wasn't entirely sure if he remembered to breathe.

Well, at least he'd be out of trouble for the next few hours.

I'd say I was being uncharitable except that he'd broken into the palace three days ago and was caught playing hide-and-seek with Khan in the queen's private garden, so… Granted, his job was to test the wards, but he was supposed to break in and then report back. Not play with Felixes.

Colette knocked at my door, a quick rap of her knuckles, before waltzing through. She had a stack of files in the crook of her elbow and gave Jameson a curious look as she came in. Her expression questioned his presence because she knew the boy kept me on edge even on the best of days.

I shrugged.

Smirking, she took the files—truly, they looked of such a weight as to crush a man's hand if carelessly dropped—and handed them forthrightly to me. "Here."

"You say 'here' as if I know what these are."

"Designs for the new equipment."

Enlightenment dawned. One of the things I'd requested of our good queen when she'd made the Queen's Own official was a better set of investigation equipment for our agents. The standard magic-detection glasses given to the police, for example, were basic in the extreme. I wanted a better version for our people. Jamie had also requested things like blood-testing kits, fingerprint kits, and the like. In the interest of communication, I wished to work with Ellie to redesign the pad, as well, to give it a longer life between charges and more enhanced features. We'd made advancements already, and they were hitting the market next month, but as soon as we had a viable product Ellie had ideas for upgrades. We were in the process of testing those, specifically a function that allowed us to send attachments and whole packets of information to each other.

Jamie called it "emails" and was so enthusiastic when I'd proposed the idea, she'd tackled me and kissed me senseless.

I smiled at the memory. We were still very much behind the curve when it came to technology in comparison to Earth, but I was determined to catch us up as much as possible. The stack of files in my hands was a jumpstart to the process and something Colette, Ellie, and Seaton had all been working on. I'd contributed as much as I could, time allowing, as of course a bulk of my time had been consumed with setting up this new branch.

"Ellie needs more data to refine things," Colette informed me while pointing at the stack. "That top file is the one she had the most questions for. By questions I mean she asked me things that went straight over my head and I honestly believe she was making up words on the spot."

"I wouldn't at all be surprised, knowing her."

"At any rate, I sacrificed you without any compunction and promised you'd have dinner with her at some point so you can talk over the particulars."

As expected of my friend. I just shook my head. "Fine. But overall, what did you think of the ideas?"

"Oh, they're quite workable. All of them. I think your attachment of pictures idea is a bit farfetched for what the pad can do now, but Ellie had some ideas, and that's what she got all excited about. I'll let the two of you hash that out. I did have some thoughts on the glasses, however. Jamie seemed to think you'd need test kits for determining what was blood and what wasn't, but couldn't we alter the glasses to do that job?"

I blinked, quite taken by this idea. "On what spectrum?"

"Well, according to the forensic books Jamie's parents sent over, there's something called a black light that will show traces of blood left behind. It shows up in a light blue glow. Couldn't we do something in the light spectrum?"

This idea was precisely why I'd sent my files around for peer review. I never knew what someone else would come up with. "Your suggestion is both brilliant and practical. Here, sit, sit, let's talk this through. Do you have an idea of how to modify the spellwork on the glasses to make detecting phosphorous particles possible without interfering with the other functions?"

"I thought perhaps like a filter that can be activated?" Colette sat at the desk with me, pulling out the file from the stack and flipping it over to the right page.

An afternoon inventing something new sounded quite a delight to me.

Report 02: New Toys

I regarded Weber from the corner of my eye, questioning the man's sanity. He looked the part of a mad scientist, alight with ideas and hyped up on too much caffeine and not enough sleep. Ever since he'd been hired into the Queen's Own, he'd been a little too pleased with himself. Mostly because he got to set up the forensic lab to his liking with state-of-the-art equipment. What coroner wouldn't be happy with that?

The icing on the cake for him, though, was that I'd several forensic medicine textbooks on a Kindle. I'd taught Weber how to use it, and the man probably hadn't slept since. The bloodshot eyes he sported rather told the story all by themselves.

He spied me as I entered the room and paused in the process of unboxing…something. It was too wrapped up in packing tape and cardboard for me to begin to say what.

"Oh good," he greeted brightly. "Hands!"

Yeah, it was official. Weber was gone. His sanity had left the building.

He made gimme gimme hands at me. "Come here, hands. I need you."

I approached, all the while looking him over. Was that yesterday's suit he still wore? "Weber, my friend, when was the last time you went home?"

"Last night. Er. I think?"

"What day is today?" I was not above testing a friend's knowledge.

"Bind Day!" he answered like a drunk, proud of himself for knowing the answer.

"You're about two days off," I informed him with a shake of my head. "So I doubt your wife saw you last night."

"Oh, she's not home. She's with her sister helping with the new baby."

Annnnnd that explained why Weber felt like he had free rein to binge-work here. What was I supposed to do with this workaholic?

He pointed to the package. "This is a new microscope. They packaged it to the point of no return. I can't get it out of the box."

Well, I could help him there, at least. And maybe slip him a sleeping draught later when there were no witnesses. "You grab the packing box, I'll lift the microscope free."

He eyed the contents doubtfully. "Are you sure? It's on the heavy side."

I just cocked an eyebrow at him. Weber, of all people, you should know my strength.

"Oh. Right." He gave me an owlish blink. "Alright, then, on three."

Weber grabbed hold of the packing carton, I grabbed the interior contents, and on three we pulled them apart. Seriously, how had they crammed this thing inside without modern machinery? Magic? Had to be magic. No other explanation I could think of.

It came free with a pop and I lifted, turned, and set it on the stainless steel table behind me.

"Great good magic, I really do forget how strong you are until I see you casually do things like this." Weber huffed as he set down the box. "I've struggled with this thing for a good thirty minutes."

"You're welcome."

I turned and looked around the room. There were two examination tables set up side by side, with cold storage in the adjoining room for storing cadavers. All of his shelves for housing equipment were arrayed along the back wall, flanked by file cabinets. It looked more and more like a coroner's lab every time I walked in here. It was even starting to smell right, that strange mix of strong cleaning products and rubbing alcohol.

"You're really making great progress setting up," I applauded him. "Are you ready to actually take on a case at this point?"

Weber recoiled in horror. "Bite your tongue! You said I had a month!"

"I was promised a month. But the world is not ideal and I don't trust promises when emergencies are a thing. I'm not saying you have to do something right now, I'm just asking if you could handle it if something did."

"Oh. No, likely not. I still have four boxes of equipment to unpack and put away before I can even contemplate the possibility."

"So, you're saying by next week, you'll be ready?"

"Quite possibly." Weber's eyes went to the Kindle on his desk with a sort of longing. Much like a goat denied a new boot to chew. "I do wish I could study all those books before we take on the next case, though. Your world's information is just so much more *advanced* in regards to medical knowledge. If I had known half of this on the past four cases I've worked, I think the outcome of the trials might well have been different."

"Well, that's why I made sure to get books to you. You're a brilliant man, Weber, I had no doubt you'd understand once you studied them all."

He put his fingers to his cheeks, like a blushing maiden, a grin curling his lips up. "You flatter me."

"It's 'cause I like you. That said, you *are* sleeping, right?"

Weber blinked ingenuously as he nodded. "I do sleep."

Uh-huh. Pull the other leg, it's got bells on it. "You like to act cute when you lie to my face, huh?"

Indignant but also chuckling, he protested, "I have neither wife nor child to distract me from studying right now. I have to take advantage while I can."

"Yeah, okay, that's fair. While I'm thinking of it, any requests for what kind of books my family can send next?"

Weber went right back to being the four-year-old child in the candy store promised any treat he could name. The transition happened in a blink, almost too fast to track. "Can they send over the designs for the machines mentioned in one of those books? The spectrometer and all of that?"

Of course he wanted the shiny new toys. Of course. I saw that coming a mile away. "Ellie's already working on it."

"Oh. Oh! She is?"

The man was funny dry drunk. I'd give him that. It made me smile at him without really meaning to. "She is. She made herself an honorary member of the Queen's Own just so she could play with new tech and have the grants to do it. I will swear to this in a court of law."

"When do you think she'll have them done?"

"Tell you what. Once you're done here, why don't you pop into her office? She's been pestering me with questions on what features these machines need to have, like specifically for you, and I have no idea how to answer her. Heck, half the time I don't understand the question. It'd be easier if you just go talk to her."

"I can do that."

"Sleep first," I advised.

Weber let out a whining sound that would not be amiss on a dog told there would be no walkies today. Seriously.

"If Ellie gets ahold of you, there will be no sleep in the foreseeable future," I warned. I meant every word—experience had taught me well. "Trust me. Get eight hours of sleep under your belt before you go visit her and, Eddy, I swear if you try to pickpocket me, I will hang you by your toes from the gate."

There was an abrupt silence from behind me. Weber tilted sideways so he could look around my body and see the mischievous teenager who'd been doing his best to sneak up behind me. Weber looked surprised to see him there, the tables having masked his approach.

Eddy grumbled, making a disgusted sound. "How do you always *know*?"

"My senses are keen enough that I can both hear and smell you." I finally half-turned to look at him. I let my amusement show because I'm evil that way. "You might move at ninja stealth, bud, but you can't do much about the smell."

An epic pout developed on his face. "You only bet me my very own library because you knew I couldn't actually manage to steal your wallet."

"Oh, you'll manage it someday. When the stars align."

"But I *want* my own library," he whined, as only a teenager could.

"Wanting things is good for you. Healthy, even. Now, can I help you with something?"

"I need books." Eddy smiled at me winsomely.

"I thought we just covered this."

"No, not a library. Study books. I'm done with the ones you gave me."

"Oh, *language* books."

"Right."

Why were teenage males so difficult to communicate with? I swear they did it on purpose. Sometimes deciphering Eddy was like riding a bicycle backward, uphill, with no seat, while gargling concrete.

I eyed his innocent expression and felt that parental suspicion stir. "You've gone through both language books already? Really?"

"Yup!"

"Did Henri test you on them?"

"Uhh...well, I meant to ask him...but he's kind of busy."

As usual, my instincts were right on the money. "Busy how?"

"He and Miss Colette are talking about blood and glasses."

Out of context, that made no sense; on the other hand, I could almost understand it. "And you didn't want to interrupt them, I take it."

"Well, Henri let me read your books."

Oh, duh. Of course that's what he'd been doing. "And

what do you think so far?"

Eddy's expression was that of a connoisseur who had finally gotten his hands on a delicacy. "Marvelous. He said I had to read them in the building, though, that they couldn't leave here. I started reading the first one. It's really good. How many are there?"

"Uh...seven, altogether." I was still very impressed this happened. Henri really must have mellowed toward Eddy if he was letting him read those. Last I checked, Henri was still willing to cheerfully strangle Eddy and kick him into the drink. Wow. Talk about progress.

"So...kiddo, you now know I'm from Earth."

He bobbed his head, eyes alight with that expression he got sometimes. The must-have-rare-knowledge look. "Henri explained before he gave me the book. Are there books on your world too?"

Ah. Of course. That was his priority. "So many books. Millions. I have quite a few with me."

"From your planet?" Eddy went off into dreamland with a sigh, like a lovelorn knight spying a lady from afar. "But it's in your language, right? I can't read it."

"Henri and Sherard created a way to translate it. You can read it."

There's puppy eyes, and then there's Eddy's version, which would put puppy eyes to shame. That expression said "can has?"

"Yes, yes, I'll fetch my Kindle and show you how to use it. Actually, that might make life easier for me. There are some textbooks on there, something that will give you a basis for my future training manuals. Is that really the only question you have to ask me?"

"I have all the questions," Eddy assured me gravely. Or he tried, anyway. He was vibrating with anticipation so he couldn't quite pull off solemn.

This guy, seriously. Still, if a Kindle's worth of books could keep him occupied and teach him simultaneously, who was I to complain? You know what, I wasn't looking this gift horse in the mouth. No sirree. I would take it and run with it.

Eddy's expression turned dreamy. "Seven case files. And another world's books. Oh, that'll be fun. So many of them."

I'd better distract him before he really got the wrong notions in his head. I snapped my fingers in front of his nose.

"Earth to Eddy. Come in, Eddy. Focus. You want more language books, right?"

The promise of new books brought him back into alignment like nothing else could. He stood almost at attention.

"Yes, ma'am!"

"Okay. I need an errand run. I've got a portfolio for you to deliver. I'll write a note and the directions on the front. You take that, and on your way back, you can stop in at the bookstore and get the next set of books you need." I pulled out my wallet and shelled out several crowns into my hand, then a bit more, just in case. Handing them to him, I directed, "Try to get an easy-to-read storybook in one of the languages too. Something you can practice your reading skills on."

Eddy was all delight because new books, yay! I personally thought him insane for studying two languages at once, but he was keeping up with them both just fine so far. Henri tested him routinely and the other agents we had in the Queen's Own tutored him and practiced conversations with him. To me, of course, it all sounded the same. That universal translation spell was strong as ever. I couldn't help him study this. But that's where my band of brothers stepped in and helped, bless them. Really, with translation spells in the world, most would have just used them instead of learning all the major languages. Eddy recoiled in horror at the suggestion. He'd rather learn. I wasn't about to stop him.

I planted a hand on Eddy's shoulder and moved him out ahead of me. I waved bye to Weber and threw a caution over my shoulder as I went. "Sleep!"

Weber waved me off like I was being ridiculous. When the man collapsed on the spot from fatigue, I hoped I would be there to tell him *I told you so* when he woke back up again.

My new office was kitty-corner to Henri's, on the main floor, and sandwiched next to Gibs'. It wasn't the largest of the offices, but I didn't need as much space as most of them, which was why I'd taken it. Besides, corner office that it was, it gave me a very nice view of the gardens. Not to mention a large window for my sunbathing cats.

I sat at my light wooden desk and penned a quick note to our uniform designer about what we'd decided on, then another sheet for Eddy so he'd have the address. Once I handed both over, Eddy was gone in a flash, humming his "new books" song as he went.

So easy to please, that one.

Alright, I'd checked in on Weber, talked with Gibs, talked with our new evidence officer—who was a spitfire, I was going to love that woman—and gotten the orders in for more desks and bookshelves. What was on my agenda next?

I'd barely reached for my to-do list when my pad beeped with an incoming message. I pulled it out, looking down at the new and improved screen. Sherard and Henri, with Ellie's oversight and blessing, had refined the design, making it lighter, more portable, and enhancing the screen so it looked less like writing with a fat crayon and more like writing with a pencil.

Regina's handwriting was distinct and crisp: *Jamie, come to my study. I have a case for you.*

Uh-oh. This must be something very important or very bad because she'd promised to give me at least another month to get the office properly set up and running before giving me any cases. I barely had a skeleton crew in here and we were still missing some essential personnel.

I mentally swore even as I penned the response. If she called for me, I had to go. I trusted her judgement that it was my department she needed.

Coming.

Report 03: James Bond

I found the queen in her study, as expected. Khan lay in a patch of sunlight on the floor in his cute chibi form, basking as only a cat with no worries could. My queen, however, had all the worries. That was evident from one look at her face. She also seemed to have rolled out of bed this morning and dressed in the first clothes at hand. While wrestling with a cat. With one hand tied behind her back.

Oh boy. Whatever this was, it was worse than I'd anticipated. I'd never seen Regina anything less than perfectly put together except on Girls' Night.

I greeted her with a short bow and a worried smile. "Need a Girls' Night?"

Regina flopped in her chair, letting her head roll against the back as if just the effort of keeping her head upright was too much just then. "If I wasn't sending you to another continent, I'd take you up on that offer."

"Uh...okay, that's definitely a first. I'm going to a different continent?"

"I've debated for a full day whether to send you or not, but in truth, no one else is better suited than you and Henri."

"The way you say that worries me. Where am I going?"

"Dolivo." She pointed me to a chair in front of the desk.

I took it, but also pulled out my trusty notebook so I could write particulars down. She wasn't kidding, that really was another continent north of us. Not that I'd ever been there. I hadn't been out of our country's borders yet.

Also, completely irreverent of me, I know, but sitting here across from her like this just suddenly reminded me of every

James Bond movie I'd ever seen. In that moment, Regina was M.

Wait, if Regina was M, who was Q? Ellie?

I had a really hard time keeping that thought off my face. I managed not to say it aloud, but my face sure needed deliverance.

Focus, me. I'm supposedly an adult. I could laugh at my own private jokes later.

"First, let me say I would not send you if I felt it best to send anyone else. But..." Regina trailed off with a grimace. "This case is very much a mystery, and I fear it might get messy in the worst sense."

I gave myself a mental slap and focused. Time to be serious. "I figured it had to be bad for you to break your promise to me. It's okay, I'm braced."

"Let me start at the beginning. You're aware that we're investing more and more in Dolivo to improve relations with them?"

"I'm aware that you have a cute boyfriend, aka the second prince of the country, and that relationships are improving quickly, yes." I gave her a cheeky grin.

Regina gave me an unamused look, lips scrunched up, but her eyes were laughing. She appreciated I could tease her. I was one of the few who dared.

"How is Cute Boyfriend, by the way?" I asked, still teasing. Mostly. I hadn't actually gotten an update from her since the last time we'd talked, when she'd confessed she'd started dating someone.

"Our courtship is going quite well, thank you." After that prim response, she tacked on, "He's quite fun to kiss."

"Awww, young love."

"Oh, stop. I'll start teasing you about Henri next."

"Henri's more fun to tease. He blushes. Just saying."

She rolled her eyes. "You're incorrigible. To you, I can admit part of the reason why I'm deploying you is because of Egon. He and I entered a business venture together in Dolivo—specifically in Haverford—that's vital to the health of both of our countries. This latest event threatens it in the worst way. He's quite upset, understandably, and pleaded with me to send my best investigator. He knows about you, you see."

Ah, now that did shed light on a few matters. "I'm extremely flattered. What's the business venture?"

"You're familiar with consumption, the illness?"

"I am." Earthians called it TB, or tuberculosis. It was deadly for many generations before modern medicine found a cure for it. Now it was preventable in my world. Not so much here. Their medicine was a good hundred years behind. Here, if you caught TB, you were walking dead. Magic could do a lot, no question, but the root of the spells had to understand the disease. If they didn't know why it damaged a human body, they couldn't make a cure for it. Much like modern medicine. TB was one of those pesky illnesses they hadn't made a counter to yet.

"We've found a cure for it."

Now she had my complete attention. I sat up so fast, I heard vertebrae pop in my spine. "Are you serious? Deployed right, that cure could save hundreds of thousands of people—"

"If not millions." Her smile turned genuine for a moment, less strained. "I know. The patented cure is a potion. At the onset of the illness's symptoms, all a person needs to do is take the potion once. They're cured at that point. We've tested this rigorously for the past six months and the cure rate is one hundred percent."

I let out a low whistle. Now that was freaking impressive, no lie.

"Egon and I pooled resources and funds to create a factory in Dolivo to mass produce this potion. Fortunately, it's low on the magic spectrum for production, so sufficiently trained journeymen can do it."

"That's awesome. Why Dolivo, may I ask?"

"Half of the ingredients needed for the potion are found in Dolivo's mountains. It was easiest—and less expensive—to put the factory right near its ingredient source."

"Makes sense."

"Egon's also very invested in bringing an economic boost into that area. It's just far enough from the sea that it doesn't see much in the way of trade. The country relies too heavily on import and not enough on export, so the economy is suffering. Building a factory there will hopefully be the right start in rectifying the problem."

Ahhh, got it. This was a two-birds-one-stone situation. They really couldn't afford for things to go wrong. It would have the worst sort of ripple effect.

"The factory is in its beginning stages of operation. It's taken six months to build it, refine the process, and actually start production. Our shareholder reports were due this month, in fact, and the liaison for it is Lady Ioana Blatt."

I noted the name. It sounded vaguely familiar. No doubt Henri would recognize it immediately.

The stress was back full force on Regina's face. I could tell every word coming out of her mouth was bitter in the extreme.

"Lady Blatt and our factory supervisor, Mattius Celto, were found in Celto's office two days ago. It is, by all appearances, a murder-suicide. Or an attempted one, at least. Lady Blatt still clings to life."

Well now, that wasn't good. I noted down names even as questions bubbled to the surface. "Why do you say murder-suicide?"

"A suicide note, with a protection ward around it, was found on the desk by Celto's hand."

Okay, that would be kinda obvious, then. "What was the purpose of the murder suicide?"

"The note claims it was a doomed affair."

The way she said that raised more questions. "Were these two having an affair?"

"That's where the questions arise. I don't see how they could be. Lady Blatt is affianced right now, and to a man she adores. I know this for a fact. Also, as far as I'm aware, Lady Blatt and Celto barely crossed paths more than a dozen times. She's an investor, not really at the factory on a regular enough basis for them to carry on an affair. Yet the note said Celto couldn't live without her and that they saw no hope for their future together. I'm..." She rubbed at her forehead. "I'm utterly confused by this."

"Could be this was entirely one-sided on his part and he lured her there under false pretenses before trying to kill her?" I offered.

Regina paused and blinked at me. "Oh. Now that's a thought. I hadn't considered that."

"I'm totally spitballing. I don't have enough facts to really guess right now. Not the first time a man's killed a woman he couldn't have, though. Sadly. Right, so you don't think this is an affair. Could be we're looking at something else. Any sign of the factory being broken into?"

"None."

"How did he attempt to kill them both?"

"With small explosion spells. I understand they did incredible damage to both them and the office."

I winced. Explosion spells? Really? Come on, there were more painless ways to die, surely. "And Lady Blatt survived this?"

"Barely. She's in the hospital now with her fiancé looking over her. We're all hanging on with the high hope she might survive this."

"Not to step on toes, but maybe I should take Vonderbank up with me? He's your healing expert, after all. Might be he can help too."

Regina gave me a nod without any hesitation. "The doctor on site has done all she can. I don't know if Vonderbank can do much more, to be frank, but I wish to exhaust all avenues. I'll give him the order myself."

I know the royal mages didn't really get along with each other, but Henri got along with all of them. Vonderbank was an unparalleled genius when it came to healing, too, hence he'd been appointed to begin with. If anyone could save this poor girl, it would be him. I wanted to give her a fighting chance.

"Anything else you can tell me?" I prompted.

"Sadly, no. I have little in the way of details, as things are hectic and confused up there." She folded her hands on the desk, knuckles white under the force of her grip. "Jamie, I want you to take my private yacht. Get up there with all speed. I believe, in my heart of hearts, that this isn't what it looks like. Celto had everything to live for. He was on the brink of becoming incredibly wealthy, as this was his potion. We'd only bought the rights to produce it."

Well, crap. I had to agree it did look weird. Who chose to off themselves on the verge of becoming a multi-millionaire? And he would be if he could cure TB worldwide. Unless something else was at play here, a suicide didn't make sense to me.

"We'll take the yacht with thanks. I promise to update you as I figure things out."

Regina relaxed a hair. Only a hair, though. "Who all will you take?"

"I'll double-check roster availability, but…Henri, Evans, Niamh, and Eddy, I think."

"Not Gibson or the others?"

"We're still setting up the office down here. I don't dare take everyone. I'll send for Weber if I need him, but I'll try to use the coroner and police up there to fill in for manpower. It's not like I have jurisdiction up there, anyway. I'll need someone with me."

"Egon has promised you power of investigation," she assured me. "But yes, please keep the local police in the loop. They will have to try the culprit up there."

Yup, figured. "I'll do so. Anything else before I take off?"

"No. I'll send more information as it comes to me."

I stood but before I left, I offered, "Obviously we can't do it now, but Girls' Night after I get back?"

Regina slumped a little, looking beyond tired. "Yes. Please."

"Consider it done." I gave her a wink, a quick bow, and

took myself off again.

The queen's study was just a short jog away from my new office building. I may or may not have hummed the *James Bond* theme song as I went. It just felt appropriate. I was back at the Queen's Own HQ within three minutes. As I entered the front door, I called out, "Avengers, assemble!"

No one got the reference except my cats, who popped out of the breakroom—they'd been napping, I had no doubt—and Henri, who appeared in his office doorway down the hall.

"What is it?" Henri asked, poised to go back into his office if I said I didn't need him.

Yeah, he'd been in research mode. I could tell from his expression. "Sorry, love, duty calls. We're to board a boat for Dolivo as quickly as we can manage it."

His dark brows drew down in worry. "I'm almost afraid to ask why."

"We've got a suspected murder-suicide up there that's endangering something that can save a lot of lives. I'll explain details as we go, but right now, pack."

Henri gave me a nod and immediately returned into his office.

Eddy popped out next with one of my case files in his hands and asked, "Who am I studying with while you're gone?"

I shook a finger and tsked him. "Weren't you supposed to be at a bookstore?"

"I got distracted by the book."

Yeah, I should have seen that coming. Eddy had a really hard time putting a book down once he started it. "Well, you better get over there quickly. You're coming with, kiddo."

At first, his expression was all elation. Then his eyes dropped to the book in his hand and I could see the open conflict. Fun trip outside the country versus book he wanted to finish. Only a true bookworm could understand the struggle.

I sympathized, really, but I wanted him to experience

other cultures and get used to international travel. He couldn't do that if he stayed at home during all of his training. "It'll still be here when you get back."

"Can't I take it with me?" he pleaded.

"No chance. Henri's very possessive of those. Now, go home and pack. Enough clothes for a week, your travel papers, and all your study books." I shooed him on with a hand. "Be back here in under two hours."

Making a face, he shrugged in agreement.

Alright, my grasshopper was sorted. Now, to get everyone else moving.

All the offices were down this hallway, meaning I could quickly fetch who I needed. Evans was in his office, so he was easy. I couldn't find Niamh for love or money, though. I finally went into Gibs' office, as I needed to update him anyway, let him know I was going and who I'd take with me.

My big bear of a friend was kneeling beside his desk, unpacking a box of files into a file cabinet in the corner.

"Gibs."

He turned at my hail and looked up, staying on the floor. "I heard you say something about going somewhere?"

Sound didn't carry all that well in this building, so I repeated the basics for him. "A case in Dolivo. Queen Regina issued this one herself. She's got a factory up there she's invested in that's developing a potion that will cure consumption—"

Gibson whistled, brown eyes flaring wide. "I'd heard rumors about that!"

"Rumors confirmed, my friend. Anyway, the factory super and one of the shareholders were found in his office, set up to look like a murder-suicide."

"Uhhh...why?"

"That is the question. The suicide note left behind claims this was a doomed love affair. It's putting the whole thing in jeopardy, though, and Regina wants us up there yesterday."

"I don't blame her. That's a lot of money and lives tied up in that factory. Who are you taking?"

I ticked people off on my fingers. "Henri, Evans, Niamh, and Eddy."

The expression of relief on Gibson's face at hearing Eddy's name made me laugh.

"Yes, I'll take the troublemaker with me."

"He's a sweet kid, really, he's just…"

"Yeah. I know. A handful."

"And he really only obeys you, for some reason."

"That's because I give him creative outlets for his wiggles. Anyway, I'm trying to leave in the next two hours. You seen Niamh?"

"No, I think she's running an errand. I'll contact her, you go home and pack."

"Can you handle newbie lunch? Or just cancel it until I'm back."

"I can handle it, don't worry. Go, go."

I gave him an analyst's salute and went out the door.

Gibson called after me, "And keep us updated!"

Him and about a dozen other people. "I'll try!"

♫ Dun dun dun-dun dun dun dun-dun~ ♪

You're going to be singing that song all the way to Dolivo, aren't you? maaaaybe

Take responsibility when you get it stuck in my head.
rejected

Report 04: Gathering Experts

Jamie came into my office, towing Evans along with her. She stayed long enough to give us the basics of the case, which sounded both problematic and intriguing. A potion that could cure consumption would indeed have a worldwide impact for the better. I absolutely did not want to see this fail.

After Jamie left to go pack, I turned to Evans, staying him with one hand. "Wait, let's discuss what to bring with us."

Evans pulled up a chair at the table next to Colette and sat immediately, his grey eyes keen. Evans wasn't a large man by stature—he ran both short and lean—but within his frame he held a powerhouse of magic. Not on the same level as a royal mage, but still a powerful individual. He was also very clever with his magic, the type to use the smallest amount of magic necessary to bring about the best result. He and I got along splendidly because we thought along the same lines.

In his smooth bass, he stated, "If this really isn't an attempted murder-suicide, then it could be any number of things. Someone could have murdered those two to cover up something else. We'll need to examine the potion, the factory, and the staff in detail."

Colette pushed aside our blood-filter designs and pulled paper and pen to her, jotting things down. "Sampling kits, evidence bags, a black box and camera to document the scene, those number placards Jamie had made up...what else?"

"I burn through notebooks during investigations, so several of those." I sat back and thought for a moment. "It's a shame our new investigation glasses aren't made up yet. But let's bring a few pairs of the standard issue for everyone else. If there have been explosions in that office, no telling what residue is lurking about. I don't want people stepping in it."

Evans gave a vigorous nod. "None of that, please. I've only seen Jamie trip into something once that somehow bypassed all her spells, and the result of that was *not* pleasant."

"I've seen her do it twice, and I don't want a repeat ever again, thank you." Just the memory of those instances gave me nightmares sometimes.

Colette gave us both a look, dark brows arched in question. "Isn't this her first time off continent?"

"Yes, I believe so, why?"

"Did anyone think to warn her how cold Dolivo is?"

I blinked at my friend and then realized no, likely no one had. Such general information was often forgotten until Jamie expressed some surprise over it. We were just so used to this knowledge. The sun is warm. Grass is green. Dolivo was incredibly cold in winter.

I mentally kicked myself and drew out my pad, scribbling a quick message to her.

Jamie, Dolivo is colder than here. Pack warm.

The response came back a moment later. *Thanks for the warning!*

There, now she was sorted. I put that aside and focused once again on making up a thorough list of what all we should take with us. I had no idea of the state of forensics in a foreign country and, quite honestly, I didn't want to show up looking ill-prepared. Or needing to borrow things they might not have. It was better for me to take everything along.

Once we felt we had a good, comprehensive list,

Evans helped pack everything up. We had things sorted quickly, as Evans was the efficient type. I sent him off to pack and almost did the same, then I second-guessed that thought. Before going home myself, it might behoove me to speak with Vonderbank. He was far more knowledgeable about medicine than I; there could be something obvious that I'd failed to consider.

Instead of heading out, I headed further in, going toward the royal mage building. I'd barely stepped foot inside the main foyer when I was forced to an abrupt halt, as Seaton nearly barreled into me.

"Davenforth! Fancy meeting you here." He paused, collecting his own balance before speaking. On this winter day, his usual red coat was absent, replaced by a thicker, fur-lined version in the same color. He was in fine spirits, too, looking quite ready to find mischief.

"Seaton," I greeted in return. "I'm in fact on my way up to speak with our colleague."

Seaton's expression turned perfectly blank. "Which one? Wait, why not me?"

"Not your expertise. Vonderbank's the man for this, I think. The queen's issued a case for us in Dolivo."

"Why Dolivo?"

I filled him in on the particulars, watching that formidable intellect gather all the facts and put the pieces together at a rapid pace. Then he pursed his lips in a silent whistle.

"This is a high-stakes case. I can see why she wanted Jamie for it."

"Quite so. I think she wants Vonderbank up there specifically to see if something can be done to save Lady Blatt, but having him on hand to consult with will be handy for us as well. I am sorry we can't request you for this, though."

Seaton's pout wouldn't have been out of place on my nephew's face after being denied a treat. "You know how much I love working cases with you two. Can't you wiggle me in somehow?"

"If I find a valid excuse for it, I'll call you in immediately, I promise. In the meantime, can you try to help efforts here? We're still recruiting personnel for the Queen's Own and taking four people out of the office right now is a bit..."

Seaton held up a hand. "Say no more. I'll check in daily and make sure they understand they can call upon me for help."

He was such a dear friend. I clapped him on the shoulder in thanks. "Good. I feel better about leaving now. It's too much to dump all this on Colette and Weber when they're still setting up their offices and labs."

"For that matter, are you still setting up your office?"

I pulled a face, much like after having bitten into too-sour fruit. "Yes."

Seaton chuckled, shaking his head. "Criminals are so inconsiderate. They could have at least waited until your office was set up."

"I'll be sure to say that to them when I catch the culprit, whomever that is." I could feel time ticking away in the back of my mind and I glanced toward the stairs. "I really must go, I have no time as it is. Keep me abreast of things here, please."

"Keep me updated on things there, too," he countered. "I want to know how this pans out."

"I will." I gave him a quick smile as I passed him, heading up the stairs.

Fortunately for me, Vonderbank was not on the third story but the second, so I only had to ascend one flight of stairs. His office door was open but I gave it a rap of my knuckles as I paused inside the threshold.

"Vonderbank?"

The esteemed mage turned, his chalk-holding hand dropping slightly as he took me in. Vonderbank was the oldest of us RMs, although still a healthy fifty-year-old man, and from one of the rarest races of men. The gargoyle blinked owl-like eyes at me, his grey wings unfurling from where they'd been tucked behind his back so one of them could give me a wave hello. Then again, his hands were both rather full.

"Why, Davenforth, hello! What brings you here?"

"A case I need your help on. Queen Regina, I believe, will give you an official request shortly, but I thought to give you a heads-up since the situation demands speed."

He blinked, tail twitching in surprise, and readily put the notebook and chalk down. "You don't say. A case?"

"Quite so. There's been a strange set of murders in Dolivo—or attempted murder, in one case. Lady Blatt—do you know her?"

"I know her family, but it's been many years since I've seen her in person. I believe she's engaged now?"

"She is. She's one of the victims in this case."

Vonderbank's jaw dropped, tail lashing so hard it threatened to topple the stool next to him. "No! Dead? That sweet, intelligent girl?"

"No, she's fighting to stay alive, but someone tried to kill her. She's in Dolivo now. Queen Regina wants you to come with us, see if there's anything more you can do to help her. I understand that a doctor is attending her, but..."

"Dolivian magic and medicine differ quite a bit from ours. There's no harm in me taking a look and aiding her if I can." He put his hands together, rubbing them briskly to rid himself of the chalk. "I'll go at once. How long has it been since she was attacked?"

"Two days."

"That's already a good sign. If she's still clinging to life, then odds improve in her favor. Where, precisely, is she?"

"Haverford."

"Oh my, quite the distance up."

He didn't seem displeased by this. But then, the only time he was ever called off palace grounds was for an emergency or to help renew wards. No doubt he would like the opportunity to take in fresh scenery. I certainly would, in his shoes, and I was a notorious homebody.

I did think it prudent to warn him. "Vonderbank, this might be...that is to say, she was hit with an explosion spell."

For the first time in our acquaintance, I saw the man perfectly speechless. After a rather decent impersonation of a landed fish, he spluttered, "She's still alive?!"

"I have the same question, how she survived but the man in the room with her didn't. Will you look into that for me?"

"Great magic, I will! I can't let such a question lie unanswered." Vonderbank scurried for his desk, muttering as he went. "An explosion spell. Who uses an explosion spell to kill? Insane, utterly insane! I'll need warmer clothes. A notebook, too, I'm sure this will be of use on the case—Davenforth?"

"Yes?"

"I assume your partner is spearheading this investigation?"

"Indeed."

His expression firmed, and on an elongated face such as his, it looked ferocious indeed. "I'll collect whatever evidence I find and note it perfectly for her. Let's catch the dastard who did this. I remember Lady Blatt to be a good, sweet girl. She didn't do anything to deserve this."

"No, she did not. Will you join us? We're sailing up by yacht within the hour."

Shaking his head, he reached for a black bag quite

similar to my own that sat on a nearby table. "No, it's best I portal up. Time is of the essence in situations like these. The royal summons can catch up with me."

This man had gained fame during a forest fire twenty years ago, saving countless lives with not only his medical knowledge, but the magical power he had to bear on the situation. If anyone understood how to respond in an emergency, it would be him. I wasn't about to disagree with him.

"Good luck, then. Keep us updated and we'll catch up with you quick as we can."

With a little half-salute, he snapped out, portaling quickly away.

I could only hope he saved Lady Blatt. If anyone had a prayer of using magic to sustain her life, then he was surely the man to send.

As for me, I had packing to do. Regardless of whether Lady Blatt lived or died, it was my duty to find out who had done this to her.

I messaged my queen as I headed back down.

I spoke with Vonderbank. He's portaling up now to see if he can help Lady Blatt.

She responded immediately. *Excellent. My summons will catch him too late, but I'd rather he go up with all speed. How goes your preparations?*

I need to pack, but we're to rendezvous in an hour. Your Majesty, one question.

Ask.

May I keep Vonderbank with us after his healing of Lady Blatt? I want his professional opinion on the potion and the factory itself. I'd like a second set of eyes.

You may keep him for as long as you both please, barring an emergency here.

Bless her for being so flexible. Technically speaking, Vonderbank was the first line of defense here in the palace. If anything were to happen to the royal family, he was the one to render immediate aid. It's why he stayed on palace grounds most of the time. For her to give him free rein on foreign soil was very generous.

Thank you.

Davenforth, I want to impress upon you that I cannot afford for this venture to fail. It has nothing to do with the money I've invested in it. I want this cure for my people.

I promise you, we'll do our best to figure this out quickly so you can get the factory back on track.

Thank you.

I understood her worry. A cure for consumption was a breathtaking proposal. I wanted it to succeed just as much. I truly hoped the death of the factory supervisor wasn't enough to derail or delay it.

If my Jamie had her way, that situation would be reversed in short order.

Jamie's Additional Report: 007

Why 007?

reasons

We were on the yacht by late afternoon. Let me tell you something, the queen's private yacht was *stylin'*. There were even enough cabins for us to all have private rooms. Really tiny ones, granted, but still.

I set up shop in the dining room, papers spread out in front of me, wishing once again for a computer. Well, technically I had one, but I couldn't print, so for this purpose it was practically useless.

Revising lesson plans was so much fun.

Too much sarcasm?

The stress of developing my department might have been getting to me. It was just a lot to coordinate and, even with all my help, there was a great deal only I could do. Lesson plans being a prime example. I was in that balancing act of wanting it all over with so I could stop stressing about it, and panicking because I wasn't ready to fully open the division.

My stress dreams had gotten really weird, let me tell you.

My favorite pest dropped into the chair next to mine and leaned against my shoulder so he could read my lesson plan. I studied Eddy from the corner of my eye, feeling this mix of amusement and sisterly affection. If someone had told me a year ago that I'd end up semi-adopting this kid who kept breaking into palace grounds, I'd have laughed hysterically. Here Eddy sat, though, quite comfortable encroaching on my personal space.

I never had a brother, younger or older. Still, I kind of treated him like a sibling, the reckless one that didn't have the brain cells to think things through. It seemed to have been exactly what he needed. His own parents wanted to throttle him most of the time. His siblings didn't know how to relate to him. I was one of the few who recognized his talent and gave him the training and outlets he needed to use it.

Eddy had latched on to me because of it. In his shoes, I would have too. He was cute, when he wasn't up to mischief, so I didn't mind having a younger brother following me about. I was a little surprised Henri had mellowed toward him, but I think it was the love of books that brought those two together. Hard to stay mad at a fellow booklover.

"What are you doing?" Eddy inquired, eyes scanning the text.

"Revising lesson plans."

"You didn't like how you planned them?"

"Mm, parts of it were rough. I did one class to test things out and it was bumpy. I'm having to adapt what I was taught to this world's cultures and technology level, and that didn't work perfectly on the first try. I had to stop and revise a couple of times right there on the spot. I'd like to get people trained enough to where someone aside from me is teaching, which means getting these lesson plans down pat."

He nodded sagely, still leaning up against my shoulder like a limpet.

Sometimes, I suspected Eddy was as starved for physical affection as he was for anything else. I ruffled his hair and got a grin in return.

"And how goes your studying?" I asked.

"Brain's not sure whether to implode or explode."

Ah, which was why he was bothering me. Got it. "Well, I arranged with the ship's captain and crew that when you couldn't take any more studying, you were to go to them. They'll teach you how to sail and navigate."

He popped up immediately, eyes so bright with joy that you'd think I'd offered him five Christmases at once. "Really? Right now?"

"Yup, right now. Go forth and conquer."

Eddy was off like a shot, air vacuuming in his wake. I

shook my head, grinning after him. This kid, seriously. Offer him a fortune and he wouldn't be interested. Give him the chance to learn something new, you couldn't keep him still. It's why he would be such a good spy in the future. The desire to know, above all else, was his motivation.

I went back to my lesson plans. Alright, how to explain this better?

"Jamie?"

I twisted in my seat to look behind me. Evans was leaning half inside the door, a concerned look on his face.

"What?"

"I saw Eddy sailing the ship...?"

"Yeah, I arranged for the crew to teach him how to sail. I promise a novice is not at the helm without supervision."

Relief flooded his face. "Oh, good. I wasn't sure if I needed to intervene or not. Your Felixes are in on it too, for some reason."

"We have a saying on Earth: Curiosity killed the cat. Satisfaction brought it back."

"In other words, they like to get into everything too."

"Story of my life, man."

A light bulb went off. I was thinking in circles, probably overthinking, but here was fresh blood right in front of me. "Hey, Evans, you busy?"

"No, why?"

I pointed to the chair near me. "Sit. Let me run something by you. I'm no longer sure if I'm making sense or not."

Evans shrugged and came to sit with me.

I hid an evil smile behind a pleasant one. He had no idea what he'd just volunteered himself for. I would not relinquish him from helping me with revisions, not until I was sure that this time they were right.

You made a grown man cry for mercy.

That's what I do.

Evans might not ever help you again.

Oh, he will. I have my ways.

Report 05: A Cure to Die For

I had never been more grateful to see dry land. It's not that I disliked ships—short jaunts were fine—but I'd never developed sea legs. After sixteen hours or so on the water, a light queasiness had settled in the pit of my stomach until even the smell of food became intolerable. I was as bad as an expectant mother. Thank everything I could name for wind spells to speed the journey along, otherwise the trip would have taken nearly twice the time. A truly horrendous thought, that.

Fortunately, I knew myself well. I'd packed several anti-nausea potions for myself and the rest, which turned out to be rather prudent, as Niamh suffered as well. We were entirely sympathetic to the other's plight and took turns about the deck, breathing in fresh air and trying to keep our stomachs under control.

The Woodland Elf was the first to scramble off the yacht and to the dock, her expression of relief unmistakable. Jameson was right behind her, head spinning this way and that as he took in Dolivo. Well, what he could make of it in the dark. It was only three hours away from dawn.

I breathed in the air, feeling it crisp and cool in my lungs, and smiled. Land. Blessed land.

A tiny paw touched my cheek.

"Henri, Henri. We there?"

"We're here," I answered Phil, gracing him with a glance. He sat on my shoulder, as was his wont, tucked in with my scarf to keep off the chill. I could just see the white of his chest and the tip of his white chin above the scarf, his eyes even more golden than usual in appearance. "Stay close, please. No one here will recognize what you are."

"Will," he promised faithfully. Then turned and scolded, "Clint, stay close."

It said something that the youngest of the bunch did not trust their elder.

For good reason, granted.

Before I forgot, again, I cast a universal translation spell upon everyone so they wouldn't struggle with a language barrier during our time here. Jamie, efficient woman that she was, gathered us all together as well as our luggage and got us moving toward the town. The dock we were on seemed to be more or less in the center, its crescent shape coming to a head near the yacht's docking.

Just as we reached the end of the wooden docks, a thought struck. Phil might not trust Clint to not wander off, but I had someone else I didn't trust. I snuck my wand out of my inner coat pocket and surreptitiously cast a spell.

Beside me, Evans choked, covering his mouth to hide his amusement. He leaned in to whisper, "Did you just put a tracking spell on Eddy?"

"I did." I had no remorse about doing so, either.

"Good thinking. I mean, I know we have Niamh, but—"

"I'd rather not turn her into a hunting dog unless required."

Evans snorted on another laugh, almost choking. "Agreed."

The nearest hotel to the docks looked reputable, with its fresh white paint and swept sidewalk. Jamie glanced around, pointing toward its door.

"Any objections?"

I shook my head. No one else seemed inclined to argue either, so she stepped sprightly up the two steps and through the door. It was only after she entered that I read the sign next to the door.

Main Street Hotel? Surely better names were to be had. Although it was a utilitarian name if nothing else.

Despite the name, it smelled like lemon and beeswax inside. The place was scrupulously clean although older in style. I hadn't seen forest green carpets since I was a young child in my grandparent's home. It was all the rage then.

The night clerk looked to be of my grandparents' age, for that matter, and half asleep on her feet. She booked us with efficiency, however. We were able to secure rooms for each person without issue and went upstairs to pass out immediately on the soft beds.

The wake-up call at my door felt like it came only five minutes later, but five hours had passed. I felt groggy in the extreme, my body out of sync with the disrupted sleep schedule. Still, I'd been a policeman long enough to be able to adjust. A wash at the sink, a shave, and fresh clothes did much to revive me. A hot breakfast served in the hotel's dining room completed the job.

By nine o'clock, we were all fed and ready to go. Jamie herded us back out the door. As a country, Dolivo was quite picturesque and known for being largely mountainous, with thick forests of pine trees, some of them primeval and untouched by human hands. Haverford sat nestled against the base of the mountains, a large lake providing both transportation and fishing for the town. It was disconnected from the main coast, sitting almost squarely inland, their only connection to the sea a long, winding river.

It was a clean-swept city from what I could see, but the streets were narrow, harkening back to its ancient roots when streets weren't built wide. A quaint town, with thatched roofs and brightly colored trim work. If this town was any closer to the coast, it would no doubt be a favorite tourist location with its looks.

There was no need to inquire where the police station might be; we spotted the sign for it across the street almost immediately upon exiting the hotel. Jamie led the way, and there was such little motor traffic on the road, we weren't at all hindered making our way across.

Like every other building on this street, the police station looked quaint and old. A two-story building of grey stone, it was on the smaller side for police stations I'd been inside. I had the feeling it was a renovated building, something taken over from a different kind of store, a feeling enhanced when a bell above the door chimed as Jamie pushed through. This had definitely been a shop at some point. The counter that immediately greeted us, barely a full stride inside, looked more like a register than anything else.

Inside smelled strongly of fresh paint, the white walls gleaming with it. The bullpen held only four desks in clusters of two, with just enough walkway around them for people to pass. A tidy place, everything in order, but the Dolivians were known for their efficiency and cleanliness. I didn't expect anything different.

The front desk sergeant, a white werefox, greeted us with a nod and inquisitive golden eyes. "Hello, may I help you?"

Jamie fished out her badge and showed it. "Jamie Edwards, Queen's Own from Kingston. We're here for the Celto-Blatt case."

"Oh! Yes, come through, everyone's expecting you. His Highness barely came in thirty minutes ago."

Excuse me? I had not been informed we'd meet any sort of prince here. We'd of course kept Queen Regina up to date on our arrival, but had she sent word ahead of us for him to meet us here?

I had no chance to ask the question. The sergeant hopped lightly off her stool and escorted us back. Not far, as it turned out, just into the next side room, which was quite narrow but accommodated a long table, several chairs, and a chalkboard mounted to the far wall. Also people. I took in two police officers wearing black uniforms, both sitting ever so slightly on the edge of their seats and looking more than a little nervous.

The prince sitting across the table from them might have had something to do with that. His entourage, which included a retainer and two bodyguards, formed a silent wall behind him.

In appearance, at least, he made for an imposing figure. You could see the Mountain Elf in him immediately, not only in the pointed ears but in his build. Not even the tailored suit could hide the muscles this man had. A hint of crow's feet lingered in his burnished copper skin, blue eyes sharp in contrast. His head swiveled immediately to take in our entrance, and there was nothing but relief on his chiseled features.

I was quite likely the only person here who had experience in greeting foreign royalty so I stepped up to take lead. Giving the man a bow, I raised my head with a polite smile. "Your Highness. We are Queen Regina's Queen's Own. May we approach?"

"Please do. I've been anxiously expecting you." He stood and came around the table, a hand extended. That I hadn't expected. "Egon Durchdenwald."

Jamie, of course, didn't hesitate a moment in accepting that hand in a firm grip. "Jamie Edwards. This is my team, Henri Davenforth—"

I shook hands as well, not surprised by the strength of his grip. Mountain Elves were famously strong.

"—Niamh ó Murchadha, Edward Jameson, and Taylor Evans."

He shook hands with us all, then waved us into the

chairs. "Please, join us. Let us explain the situation at hand. With me are the responding officers to the scene, Officers Bauer—"

Bauer was a heavyset brown werebear, his nose twitching as he took us in, eyes a bit wide for some reason.

"—and Koch."

Koch waved a friendly hello from her chair. It wasn't often I met a gnome, but Dolivo's population had more than their fair share of them. Her flaming red hair was up in a tidy bun, and she seemed the only one unfazed by all the people in her police station.

"Pleasure to meet you." Jamie flashed them a smile. "I know time is ticking. Let's get to it, if you don't mind. I only got the basics before sailing up here. What can you tell me?"

As we found seats around the table, Prince Egon took it upon himself to start the explanation.

"This area is one I'm invested in revitalizing. You're aware of the factory's purpose? Good, good. It was put here partially to create jobs, partially because half the ingredients for the potion are found in the nearby mountains. Logistically, it just made sense. I've personally invested quite a tidy sum into the building of the factory, as has Regina. We're not the only shareholders—six others have also invested heavily in it."

I took notes as he spoke, writing quickly in the small notebook I kept on me. Details like this often made or broke a case.

"Might I have a list of all those shareholders?" Jamie asked.

"Yes, of course." Egon turned his head toward the retainer standing just behind him. The woman immediately drew out a paper from the leather portfolio clutched in her hand and passed it across the table to Jamie.

He'd come prepared, at least. That was always helpful.

Jamie took it but prompted him. "I understand Lady Blatt was also a shareholder."

"She was indeed. Lady Blatt is very active in causes. She invested in this with the hopes of curing areas afflicted by consumption. She took on some of the work that she didn't need to, all to further it along. Part of that was gathering the shareholder reports for the rest of us."

Ah, I had wondered about that part.

"I don't…" Prince Egon lifted a hand to his forehead, rubbing there as if this whole debacle pained him. "I don't understand what happened. Celto and Lady Blatt barely knew each other. The idea that the two of them were carrying on some love affair is absurd to me. I don't know if I can believe it."

"I believe nothing until I have evidence of it." Jamie turned to the officers. "You were both first responders on scene?"

"Correct," Koch confirmed with a firm nod. "The place was a mess when we first stepped in. Factory workers were there before us, one of them administering healing charms to Lady Blatt as fast as he could put them on her. Might well have saved her life. That and the protection charm she wore."

I took note of this and leaned around Jamie to ask, "What protection charm?"

"Standard issue at the factory. The minute anyone enters the door, they don a protection amulet that will protect them from the basic things: fire, falling objects, the usual hazards found in factories. I think that's also what helped protect Lady Blatt from the blast. Not enough to ward her from it altogether, obviously, but she's breathing, which says something to me."

Yes, to me as well. "Mister Celto's charm failed?"

"Wasn't wearing one that we could find," Bauer

corrected. "He'd taken his off while in the office, we think. Hard to prove that, though. Area around his desk was just kindling, nothing but debris and scorch marks."

Ahh, how interesting. I made note to look for that charm.

Jamie was also writing notes at high speed. "You said the factory workers found them. They heard the explosions?"

Koch shook her head. "No, no one heard anything. From the timing of it, looks like this happened before people reported to work. The supervisor—Celto—was supposed to be at an early morning meeting. When he didn't show, someone went up to get him and that's when they discovered the two. An alarm was sent up and people rushed Lady Blatt to a hospital. Bauer escorted them there."

"I did," he rumbled. "Helped carry her myself. She was in bad shape, barely breathing, and we're all praying she makes it."

Jamie and I shared a look. With that many people in the room, the scene had no doubt been disturbed past saving, but they'd been trying to save a life. I couldn't fault them for their response.

Egon picked up the thread once more. "There was a spell on the room to contain the explosions and dampen the noise, giving reason to why it wasn't detected before that point. We're at a loss as to how to handle this. You must understand that the entire operation is in jeopardy. The loss of two people normally wouldn't affect things this much, but Celto was the one who invented the potion."

Queen Regina had mentioned this. "Is that how he gained position of supervisor?"

"That was part of it. He was very invested in making sure his potion was made and distributed well. I couldn't think of anyone more qualified to oversee operations, so we hired him on the spot to manage things."

"Makes sense," Evans allowed. "Your Highness, I must ask just because of the name—Celto isn't a name I would think is from this country?"

"No, indeed, he's from—or was from, I should say—Itauen."

Ah, the smaller country just south of here. It was an island country and one I'd vacationed in once. Quite a lovely area. That did raise another question, however. "Why would he come up here to sell the potion process?"

"As he explained to me, importing half the ingredients necessary for the potion raised the costs significantly. If he could put a factory right near the source, it made it much cheaper and readily accessible to the poorer class."

It made sense. In his shoes, I'd have approached the prince for the same reason.

Koch tacked on, "He was a good sort, Mr. Celto. Always a smile on his face and a ready word of kindness for the townspeople. We all had a good impression of him. I can't understand the suicide note he left behind. It really doesn't make sense to us, as he didn't give any sign of being heartbroken or troubled about things. Rather the reverse—he was celebrating because we were so close to shipping out the first batch of the potion. The man was about to become very, very wealthy. This suicide-murder, taking Lady Blatt with him, it just doesn't strike my cop's instincts as true."

Jamie and I shared another look before she spoke.

"On that, I have to agree, Officer. This smells. And it's not fried chicken."

Report 06: Odds of Survival

I sent Niamh and Eddy ahead of me to figure out people's patterns, where they'd gone and such. Witnesses were extremely unreliable about this sort of thing. People noticed things, sure, but often either forgot or misremembered some aspect of it. If Niamh could figure out where both Lady Blatt and Celto were the morning of the attack, where they were coming from, and what route they took to get there, it might help us figure out what went down. If nothing else, give us a better timeline.

It was one of my proud mama duck moments. Niamh was now knowledgeable and confident enough to go investigate on her own. Not only that, I could trust Eddy with her. Well, I gave Eddy the patented look of Behave or There Will Be Consequences before he left, but that was just a given.

Prince Egon was neck deep in legalities, so I left him at the station. I went straight for the hospital where Lady Blatt even now struggled to survive. I had cats in tow, which got its usual share of strange looks. Especially with them in heated vests, their badges hanging by their collars. No one really knew what to make of a cat, much less of a police cat.

The hospital was not, by any definition, large. Two stories tall, it was made of cool grey stone and honestly looked more like a church than anything. The bell tower at the front probably had something to do with that impression. Then again, half the town reminded me of something other than its current purpose. I got the feeling that people here constantly repurposed buildings instead of building new.

Stepping inside, I was greeted by a receptionist behind

a thick wooden desk that looked like it had survived two world wars. At least. She blinked up at me, then the cats, then back at me like she was ready for rabbits to pop out of my ears next.

I flipped my badge out of my pocket and showed it to her. "Jamie Edwards, Queen's Own, here from Kingston. I'd like to see Lady Blatt."

"Oh! Yes, we were told you would stop in. Please, come this way." She popped up and skirted around the desk with commendable speed, which was impressive considering she was not a small woman. As she moved, she called ahead to another white-uniformed nurse. "Find Doctor Ratliff for me and tell her to attend to Lady Blatt's room."

Her colleague gave her a wave of acknowledgement before turning and hurrying off.

The hallways were stone slab as well, the walls white and looking their age, but I could smell the strong scent of lemon and soap, so it was clean. I followed the receptionist while taking the place in, getting my bearings as I no doubt would be repeating this trip. Hopefully for good reasons.

"Lady Blatt has been stabilized," she reported to me over her shoulder. "We're all in fear for her, however. She's not showing any signs of waking up. I personally hope the young lady makes it. She has such a sweet fiancé and he's taking this whole thing terribly, as one would expect. He's in the room with her now."

First I'd heard the fiancé was on site. "He's here?"

"Yes, has been since yesterday. He came up immediately when he was informed of the news. Her parents are in poor health, or so I'm told, so he's regularly updating them as he can about her condition. Such a sweet young man. It's very apparent this is a love match." Her mouth pursed in aggravation. "I don't believe for one second in that rumor she was carrying on with Mr. Celto. Slander, that's all that is."

I loved free gossip. Made my detective heart go fuzzy.

Lady Blatt's room was at the end of the hallway, which made sense; elevators weren't common in this world. Patients like her that weren't at all mobile would be kept on the main floor. The nurse opened the door for us and went ahead, her tone gentling as she spoke to the occupants inside.

"Lord Stewart? RM Vonderbank? You've a visitor, my lords."

"Visitors?" a rough baritone returned, sounding beyond exhausted.

I knew this tone well. It belonged to people in fear of heartbreak, of losing someone precious. It spoke of sleepless nights, of food choked down, of pain and regret. I already had a good impression of this man before laying eyes on him because he cared deeply. It was all in his voice.

I stepped through and gave a quick glance about to get my bearings. The room wasn't large, this wasn't some VIP ward, but again was kept very clean. A single window had been cracked open to let some fresh air in and I could smell the promise of rain on the wind. A single bed was in the middle of the room, various charms attached to the wall to monitor the patient and set off alarms, much like the monitors on Earth. A cot had been shoved along the wall under the window, no doubt for the fiancé, although no one was in it now.

Two things made an immediate impression. Lady Blatt lay on the bed, swathed so thickly in bandages it was a wonder she wasn't mistaken as a mummy. I could barely see skin, her fair hair in a thick braid over her pillow, her chest so still it hardly moved. Was she breathing? Oh, okay, I could hear the pained rattle of it. Wow, she was in bad shape, and I hadn't expected anything good.

The man sitting at her bedside very carefully had a hand on one of hers, slumped with exhaustion and looking up at us with serious panda eyes. I didn't think he'd slept since he'd heard about the attack. On a good day, he was likely handsome. Today, his tie hung like a crooked noose around his neck, his copper skin looked grey and wan, and his dark eyes were rimmed in red like he'd been crying recently. In his shoes, I would have been.

I could totally see why the nurse was talking to him in that gentle tone, like she was approaching a wounded animal. "Lord Stewart, I'm Jamie Edwards, Queen's Own. Queen Regina sent me up to investigate the attack."

For the first time, I saw a little spark of life come back into him. My arrival meant something and he latched on to it like a drowning man. "I'm so relieved to see you. Thank you for coming. Whatever aid I can give you in solving this mystery, please inform me."

"I certainly have a lot of questions, and I'll need everything you can tell me."

"First,"—I turned to Vonderbank, who was carefully checking on something—"how is she?"

Vonderbank didn't so much as glance up. "Do allow me a moment; I'm focused on an intricate spell. I'll update you shortly."

Fair enough. Keeping her alive was the priority. I drew Stewart closer to me so I could talk and not distract Vonderbank. "These are my Felixes, Clint and Tasha. They're...think of them like familiars. They often help me in investigations. I'd like for them to take a good sniff around the room, see if they pick up anything from her or her effects."

Stewart looked at Clint, who was draped over my shoulder, in askance but he still nodded. With Tasha being pure black, the purple Clint probably did look odd to him in comparison. "That's fine. I think I've heard of them? Queen Regina has one like them."

"You're correct, she does. Hers looks different. Jules Felix experiments with colors in every generation." To the cats, I requested, "Do your magic, guys. Just don't get in Vonderbank's way."

They gave me nods before leaping lightly to the floor and then moving off.

The nurse stepped out, drawing my attention, and conferred briefly with someone outside before a woman in a white coat and "doctor" written all over her stepped in.

I introduced myself, patient with this process.

"Doctor Ratliff, and I'm relieved to see you. This is a terrible business." Ratliff looked to be on the younger side, not freshly graduated but not far out of medical school either. She also looked like she could use about three days of sleep or a gallon of coffee poured down her throat, either one. How much sleep had she lost trying to keep this patient alive?

Doctor Ratliff was immediately distracted by Vonderbank. "What is he doing?"

"I honestly have no idea."

"You, sir, what are you doing?"

Vonderbank turned his head a little. "Sorry if I'm stepping on toes. I'm an expert in such matters, one might say."

"If you can save my patient, I don't care who you are, but what are you doing?"

She saw something that made her curious and forgot about me entirely as she went for her patient.

Two doctors were better than one, as the saying went. I let her by and refocused on Stewart. "My lord, it's a bit crowded in here. Why don't we step into the hallway and let them work?"

He gave a tired nod and followed me out, although we kept the door open. Just in case.

I pulled out my handy notebook and started in on the questions. "Tell me about you and Lady Blatt first. How long have you two known each other?"

"Years and years. We were in the same school together as children, that's how we initially met. We were always very fond of each other. Playmates. When we grew to adults, that's when our relationship changed. I asked to marry her, of my parents and hers, and no one was either surprised or objecting. We've had a fairytale romance until—" He choked off, eyes bright as he looked away.

He was visibly fighting for control and I wanted to give the man a hug so bad. He seriously needed one just then. "For what it's worth, I'm very sorry to see her in this state. Queen Regina sent RM Vonderbank up here because we want her to survive, first and foremost."

"I appreciate that very much, Agent Edwards. Thank you."

"I can also promise I will do my best to get to the bottom of this. Now, there was a suicide note on scene that suggested Celto was in a relationship with your fiancé?"

Stewart was shaking his head before I could finish the question. "I know she wasn't. The suicide note doesn't make any sense at all. If Celto felt that way for her, it was entirely one-sided and he had no business taking her down with him. Ioana has seen that man face to face perhaps a half dozen times. It was always business that made them meet. I accompanied her to half of those meetings. They had no *time* to form that kind of attachment."

"Fair enough." I was glad he had such faith in her. I jotted that information down. "So this was one of those random meetings where you didn't come with her?"

"Correct. It was entirely for personal reasons. My little sister is also getting married soon, and I stayed behind to help her prepare for the move. I wish now I'd come. Ioana was only supposed to be up here a day, two at most. It wouldn't have meant anything in the long scheme of things."

"What precisely was she up here for?"

"The shareholder quarterly reports were due. She'd come up to tour things with her own eyes, get a feel for progress, and gather the reports to send to everyone else. Ioana has never been much for letting someone else manage her business affairs. She prefers to keep her finger squarely on the pulse."

Smart woman. She was less likely to get cheated that way. "So her meeting with Celto early in the morning at the factory was just to get the reports?"

"Yes. It wasn't the first time they'd met before the factory opened."

This was scheduled. Got it. If that's the case, she might well have walked in of her own accord without realizing anything was amiss. Poor girl.

His eyes searched mine. "You don't believe she and Celto

were carrying on an affair, do you."

"I harbor doubts, shall we say. I have yet to meet anyone who believes it, and that tells me a lot. I think something else went down that morning, although I'm not sure at this point what. Tell me, did she have any enemies?"

"No. Well, not anyone who would go to these lengths. Petty school rivalries, that's all, and Ioana hasn't dealt with them in years."

I'd come back to that if I ran out of leads. He was likely right, if she hadn't had contact with those people in years, but you never knew. "Anyone trying to stop the progress of the potion up here?"

"No, not at all. People were very excited and invested in its success. It's part of why Ioana kept tabs on things personally. She was very enthusiastic about this potion."

This wasn't giving me much to go on.

"You can't think of a single person who would want to harm her?"

"I've racked my brains over that very question. I truly cannot." Stewart passed a hand over his face, looking beyond exhausted. "I can only assume it was an enemy of Celto's who brought this attack."

He might be right. I'd see, one way or another. "I'll be in town several days while we investigate this. For now, I want you to try and rest. You've got not one but two royal mages up here—"

Stewart blinked at me. "Two?"

"Henri Davenforth being the other. I have a full team dedicated and trained for this sort of investigation, and we'll do everything we can to get to the bottom of it. I'll have Vonderbank put up a protective ward around this room before we go, so you can rest assured that whoever did this can't try again."

I really thought for a moment he might cry on me. His voice was raspy, tears on the point of spilling over as he spoke.

"Thank you so much. I've been in fear of that very thing. The police routinely check on us, but…"

"Trust me, we won't give this sick bastard the opening they need to succeed. Your fiancée is tough, tough enough to survive. We'll help her along as much as we can."

Vonderbank poked his head out and gave us a smile. "Indeed, and I think she might recover fully."

Oh, now there was good news. I turned sharply to face him. "You were able to help?"

"I was. Please, both of you enter."

Stewart blasted right past me and into the room, for which I didn't blame him. I did see that Lady Blatt wore fresh bandages, and this time I could see skin. Her face at least. She looked bruised and her skin was shiny with surface burns, but she was breathing better. That painful sounding rattle had eased. Just what had Vonderbank done?

Vonderbank looked beyond pleased, his wings rustling in a gleeful way. "First, thanks and credit go largely to Dr. Ratliff. She's given Lady Blatt a very good chance of recovering from this. She not only stabilized the patient beautifully but kept all possibility of infection at bay. I would not have been able to do nearly as much if not for the patient's condition upon my arrival."

Dr. Ratliff might have been blushing. I would have been, in her shoes.

"Now, that said, I was able to do a few things to boost her healing. I've applied three healing spells to her skin that keep the area moisturized—very important for burns—trigger her immune system, and accelerate healing. It's why we were able to remove some of the bandages, as they'd only interfere with the spells at this point. The spell I just applied was to accelerate healing. She finally grew stable enough I could use it." Vonderbank drew Stewart in closer and pointed. "See how the skin is slowly turning from that angry red to a softer pink? The minor burns will close entirely by morning."

Stewart, I swear to heaven, took the first full breath since I'd met him. Relief was not a powerful enough word to describe his emotions in that moment.

"I see it. Thank you so much."

"I'm not done. I was also able to give her a— Hm. How to explain this in layman's terms. Think of it as a balloon spell. I've inserted that in her lungs to help her breathe without making it such a struggle. Dr. Ratliff did an excellent job in surgery putting her internal organs back into place, but there was significant damage on her right side. I've applied several healing spells there with the hope of helping that along. I think there's every chance she might actually be able to eat something soft by the end of next week."

"Eat?" Stewart stared at him with wide eyes. "You think she'll awaken enough to eat on her own?"

"Oh, no doubt of that. As I said, she's in remarkably good condition, all things considered. I'll stay nearby and visit her daily, boost her as I can. If she doesn't wake up by midweek of her own accord, I'll be quite surprised."

Holy crap on a stick, was he serious? This woman had taken the equivalent of a small bomb to her torso, and he thought she'd wake up in three or four days?

Magic, man. Magic was awesome.

In a more cautionary tone, Vonderbank added, "I fear that it will take a good half a year or more to truly regain full health again. I can put her back on her feet, but the nerves are very delicate things and they'll need to settle after such massive trauma. She'll need to rest and take life at an easy pace for the next six months at least."

"She'll live," Stewart choked out. "That's all I care about. Whatever she needs, I'll be there to help her."

Good answer. Man, I see why she loved him. Stewart was a really good guy.

"Thank you so much." Stewart was crying now, openly, and aside from wiping away the tears, he didn't seem at all embarrassed by his own reaction. "Thank all of you. You've worked so hard for her sake and I cannot express how much I appreciate it."

"You are very welcome." Vonderbank put a hand on his shoulder and leaned in a little. "Now, you go rest. It won't do any of us any good if you collapse next."

"I've tried. I can't close my eyes for more than a moment."

"I'll draft a sleeping potion for you. But rest and eat, so you have the strength to support her as she heals. She'll need that from you. Alright?"

Stewart nodded jerkily, sniffling, but gave a game smile. "Thank you."

"Good. Now, I must confer with Agent Edwards for a moment, and then I'll return and put that ward in place."

Oh? Did he find something interesting? I followed him out into the empty hallway like a dog hoping for a treat. Clues, please. Need clues. Please insert clues here.

The cats followed me out, as did Dr. Ratliff, which was interesting. Why?

Vonderbank stood very close to me and said in a low tone, "I've no doubt your Felixes have picked up on some of this, as they were paying very close attention to her wrists and ankles—"

"Bad sniffy," Clint reported to me before stretching up on his hind legs and demanding uppies.

I picked him up out of sheer habit, but my attention was on Vonderbank. Bad sniffy sounded promising. Tasha parked herself at my ankle, sitting like a guard dog.

"Lady Blatt had the remnants of binding spells on her wrists and ankles. Dr. Ratliff assured me those were removed before she saw her. Or at least, the worker who found her saw no restraints on her when discovered."

"Ooooh." I didn't mean to sound like a child with a new toy at hearing that, but this was the kind of intel that made cases sometimes. "How high level is this?"

"Not something a hedge wizard could do, certainly. Not that kind of spell. You're looking for a proper magician. Also, I'm informed that the position of Lady Blatt in the room was very odd. Dr. Ratliff, do explain."

I turned my attention to her.

"Lady Blatt was on her side, her head tilted away and toward the door when she was found."

Dr. Ratliff looked both ways in the hallway, saw no

one, and then plopped down. She oriented herself on the floor, lying on her side with her head turned away from me, arms together and knees scrunched up. It looked exactly like someone who had been unconscious and propped up in a chair, and had fallen out of it.

I did a very quick sketch of that position, the wheels turning in my head. "This doesn't look like she was there under her own power. I understand she was supposed to be in the office for a meeting, so was she caught in the building and then restrained? Any sign of that?"

"There was no indication of how she came to be in the room. We can only tell you how we found her." Dr. Ratliff popped back up lightly to her feet again. "The damage was entirely to her front and right side, as she wasn't laying precisely on her left side. She was tilted outward a little, half on her back."

"That's a very awkward angle, alright. No wonder her wounds are like this." I scratched at my cheek with the end of my pencil, thinking hard. "This gets more interesting by the second. Tell me more about this charm that protected her."

"She had a personal protection charm around her neck. It's standard issue at the factory. People are required to don it upon gaining the door." Dr. Ratliff ticked things off on her fingers. "It protects against falling objects, burns, chemical spills, and impacts. Not designed for this kind of explosion, so of course it couldn't stop the attack against her completely."

"But it mitigated most of it, hence she's still breathing." Lady Blatt was going to bless herself later for putting that on. "I wonder why Celto wasn't wearing one?"

"He likely didn't feel the need with the factory quiet." Dr. Ratliff shrugged sadly. "Otherwise we'd be having a very different conversation."

"Shame. Okay, you two deserve all the praise. I'm glad I can report good news back home and say Lady Blatt will most likely survive this. Thank you. Is there anything else you can tell me?"

Dr. Ratliff shook her head. "I wish, but no, that's as much

as I understand of the situation."

Vonderbank tacked on, "I'll monitor things here and free you to work. Rest assured, I won't leave until I see that young lady eating properly and know she's well on the mend. I'm quite invested in this now."

"Thank you, truly. I don't want to leave her unguarded, especially when I don't even know why she was attacked in the first place. I'll leave this situation to you. Just keep me posted."

"You do as well, Edwards. I'm thirsty for answers."

"You and me both, sir." I put my notebook away, one-handed, as Clint was apparently not interested in putting his delicate paws down on cold stone floor. Then I had to bend and scoop up Tasha, who scrambled right back into her usual pocket. I've had to change coats to larger front pockets so the Felixes could still fit. You would not believe the whining when they outgrew the other coat pockets. You'd think I'd threatened to skin them or something, that's how much wailing went on. "I'm heading to the scene of the crime next. Maybe something there will tell me what in the devil went on here."

"Good luck?" Vonderbank offered.

"Oh, I'll take it, trust me."

Jamie, I do protest this. Why wasn't I invited to go along?

I told you why.

I know, but still. I wanted to play too!

You don't think three royal mages for this case would've been overkill?

No.

I can literally hear the pout in that word.

Report 07: Deceptive Clues

> I don't like it when clues try to lie to us. I take that personally.
> *It's not nice of them, that's true.*

With Jamie heading for the hospital, Evans, Phil, and I turned our attention to the deceased Celto. We trooped down the worn stone stairs of the police station into the morgue. I couldn't imagine hauling a dead body down these narrow stairs, but upon reaching the base, I spied a door leading outside. Ah, so they had an easier entrance. That made much more sense.

The morgue was clearly not in use much. Most traffic that came through here would be accidental deaths, as murders were practically unheard of in this smaller town. The room was tiny, barely large enough to hold a table, a staging table for evidence finds, and four coolers built into the wall for body storage. We pulled on gloves before Evans and I brought out Celto's corpse and transferred him to the table with minimum fuss.

Or I should say, what was left of him.

Evans let out a low whistle as his eyes swept over the man from head to toe. "What a terrible way to go. Why would anyone choose to commit suicide like this?"

"Those who are in that kind of pain, enough to take their own life, rarely make sound decisions." I shook my head as I made the same quick study. "This, though...I agree this seems strange. The man was skilled enough to create a potion that has thwarted the rest of the world and yet he chose this violent method of death? Surely there were easier, less painful methods he could have selected from."

"I would think so." Evans gave a grunt. "Well, let's get to it. How can I assist you?"

"Turn your attention to his effects and that suicide note for now. I wish to collect samples from him."

"Samples...?" Evans' expression was perfectly blank for a moment before he took my meaning. "Oh, for toxicity reports? You think something will be left that isn't altered by the explosions?"

"I believe so. We handled something similar to this once—a car bomb—and it didn't unduly affect the blood or tissue in the legs. Oddly enough, it didn't even erase bloody fingerprints."

"Ahhh. Right, that charms case of yours and Jamie's. Alright, I'll look over the clothes, then. Phil, want to assist?"

Phil was quite happy to head that direction and away from the very gruesome corpse. I couldn't fault him. I'd rather handle the clothes myself. Still, needs must. I bent to it with diligence.

No one took just one sample when handling cases like this. The odds of a sample being accidentally corrupted were there, of course, but also the tissue affected from the epicenter of the blast would differ from something gathered from say, the hands or the feet. I took several samples, labeling them as I went, and put them in neat rows for later testing. I could do some simple tests here and now, but I'd need the use of a lab later to do a more rigorous examination.

Some might question why I bothered to do such a thing when the method of death was so clear. However, we didn't know much at all about Celto. Was he suffering from any sort of health issues? Was he intoxicated when he chose to commit suicide? Was he under the influence of anything at all? A toxicity report could tell me something of the man, and possibly more of his state of mind, at the moment of his death.

All I knew of him at this point was that he was

supposedly twenty-four, a known potions master, and from Itauen.

If being in this business had taught me anything, it was to never take anything at face value.

The angle of the explosion piqued my curiosity. If he'd used a spell, as I imagine he had, then the worst of the damage would be reflected in his hands and arms. Even if he'd spelled a charm, he would have still had to hold it. Instead, I saw the majority of the damage in his chest and stomach cavity. His hands were relatively intact, all told. That did not make sense to me, and I couldn't think of a single explanation for it offhand.

I could hear my Felix behind me make a sniffing sound, which usually prefaced something astute on his part.

"That doesn't smell right," he announced in his high voice.

I paused in capping the bottle, turning to look. "What doesn't?"

"Suicide note." His nose wrinkled, whiskers twitching. "Smells of magic."

Evans turned immediately, dropping what he was doing, and picked up the note. "There was a ward about it, right?"

"There was, yes. Is that what he's smelling?" I tilted to look at it, my eyes narrowing in strain. It took a moment longer than it should have—the spell was incredibly clever and subtle—but I soon saw something I should not have.

"This is bespelled!" Evans shared an astonished look with me.

"Well, now, that casts doubt on everything. Time to run a diagnostic spell, I think."

"I think that's your department more than mine."

Fair enough. I quickly finished bottling my sample, set it aside, and took the note from Evans. I put it back on the table, away from the clothes and other effects, drawing out a fresh journal in order to run a diagnostic spell upon it.

Even as I examined it, I couldn't help but read over the text of the letter. It was the usual verbiage of this situation—Celto couldn't live without her, couldn't see a future together, it was better to be united in death…. It scanned fine, but the words felt cold and without meaning. Much like a script of what should be said instead of embracing any kind of emotion or truth.

Phil hopped lightly onto my shoulder, Evans coming around to stand at my other side, both peering at the journal in my hand.

The answer was quick and decisive.

"Well now," Evans murmured, tone enlightened. "That does make more sense of this."

For Phil's sake, I explained, "The letter has been bespelled so the handwriting will match with Celto's. He didn't write this. Good catch, Phil, this was not obvious at first glance."

He preened himself, looking entirely pleased. As he should.

"I think we better tell Jamie."

Evans was already pulling his pad from his pocket. He was correct—this changed the situation entirely, and it would change the questions my lover would have for the witnesses. This wasn't a murder-suicide attempt anymore.

This was something else entirely.

After two rings, Jamie's voice answered with a brisk tone.

"You three couldn't have already found something."

"Phil did," Evans corrected with a grin at my Felix. "You can thank his nose. The suicide note was faked."

I heard a sharp intake of breath from her and then the sound of her footsteps came to an abrupt stop.

"Nooo," she said, intrigued. *"Do tell."*

I leaned a little into Evans' side in order to elaborate.

"The spell on the ink was such to copy another's handwriting. Celto's, presumably. He didn't write this. Also of note was that the spell was so clever, so subtle, I could barely see it with the naked eye. It was very well done."

"*Ooh, the plot thickens. So whoever did this is very good with magic, eh? Noted. Well, gents, this changes the whole game. We've got a straight up murder and attempted murder on our hands.*"

"From what I've heard, almost everyone will agree this makes more sense."

"*Oh, for sure. No one has thought the jilted lover suicide thing made any sense. I was questioning it even before you called because there's lingering magic around Lady Blatt's wrists and ankles. She was restrained, but the restraints were gone by the time she was discovered. That clearly couldn't have been done by Celto, so there had to be a third body in that room.*"

Restraints? That one word opened up possibilities in my head, and I turned sharply back to the body. A quick reveal spell told all. Well, well, well, would you look at that. I saw magic around his wrists and ankles. Now the angle of the blast made entirely too much sense.

"Celto was restrained as well. I can tell from his wrists and ankles. I had puzzled over the angle of the blast, as the damage was concentrated on his chest area. How was that possible without impacting the hands? Now I know they weren't in the way of the spell to begin with."

"*Oooh, then that settles it. This is definitely murder. Now the question is, who would try to murder these two and benefit from it? Were they just trying to get Celto, and Lady Blatt was there at the wrong time? Did the plan change on the fly to include her so it didn't look weird? Was she also a target from the very beginning? I have so many questions and not enough answers.*"

Evans and I shared a speaking look. She was quite happy about this, that was clear from her tone. But my darling loved a good mystery so neither of us was surprised.

"We'll return to examining things here, but I thought you should know."

"*Thanks, Evans, you're right. That changes this whole ball game. I definitely will be asking different questions because of it. Keep me updated.*" She blew a kiss and hung up.

Evans lifted an eyebrow in amusement. "I assume that kiss at the end was intended for you."

"Well, it certainly isn't yours," I drawled.

He just snickered, shaking his head. "It's just as well you eventually realized you love her, Davenforth."

"Why's that?"

"Because Jamie has long since decided you are her favorite person. She wasn't going to let go of you easily."

She'd told me that once, how she loved and appreciated every friend she had in this new world, but I was her favorite. How that came to be I cannot fathom. I did, however, have every intention of capitalizing on it.

Primly, I responded, "It is my privilege to be regarded as such."

"That went straight to your head, didn't it?"

I didn't deign to reply. We had work to do, after all.

Turning back to the corpse, I reluctantly focused on it instead of my lover. Alright, so Celto was murdered. There were too many things that no longer added up. Celto could hardly restrain himself, place a bomb against his own chest, and then remove the restraints after he died. Now, with this new frame of mind in place, what had I overlooked?

Like Jamie, with this information, the questions I was asking of the body had just radically changed.

There wasn't much hair left that was undamaged, but I found some on the very back of the skull that I could tease free and put into a jar. Hair was a wonderful source from which to test. Even as I worked, carefully manipulating the head and such to avoid damaging the corpse further, I made a silent vow to the man on the table.

I might not know in this moment who had murdered him, but one way or another, I'd find out.

Whoever had done this wouldn't get away with it.

Report 08: Potions Done Dirty

The factory showed many a sign of new construction. There was no landscaping around the perimeter, and the trees at the base of the mountain had obviously been cut back in order to make room for the building. It was quite possibly the largest building I'd seen so far up here, a honking three stories of light brick with a secondary jut out that was shorter, and clearly meant for office space. As I got out of the taxi, I took in the smoke coming out of the massive chimneys with surprise. It was in operation? Even with its main supervisor down?

Uhhh...well, okay then. Not sure how I felt about that.

Niamh lingered near a side door, leaning against the building with her feet crossed at the ankle. Eddy was right there with her and looking pleased with himself. I gave it fifty-fifty odds that expression would mean trouble for me later. I was glad she'd kept tabs on him, though.

I tried to pay up with the taxi driver, but he refused politely, saying that whoever helped to investigate this sorry business would get free rides from him. I thanked him instead and then off-loaded, setting down cats as soon as I was free of the vehicle. Only to abruptly shiver. It was definitely cooler up here than it had been in town. Or maybe it felt that way because the wind had a distinct nip to it.

"Jamie," Eddy greeted happily, skipping down the slope to meet me. "I found all sorts of interesting things here."

"Did you? Like what?"

He rattled things off happily. "There's six different doors, about a dozen ways to enter—some of the windows don't have latches—nothing but a basic security alarm and that's only on the main floor— Oh! And the main office is on the second floor and someone nailed it shut. New nails, very shiny."

Bless my little reformed thief. That's precisely the kind of information that helped me investigate. I reached out and patted his head.

"Good brains. Such good brains."

He beamed up at me. "That helps, right? Your notes said that knowing all points of entry is important in investigating."

"It helps so much. I now have possibilities of how someone got in here. Niamh, how about our two victims?"

She pointed to the road I'd just used to come up. "They both came up from there, which isn't surprising. That's the only road that leads to town. Lady Blatt was staying at the only upscale hotel in town and came directly from there to here. Celto has an apartment in town near the market, and he also came directly from there to here. I saw signs that he'd visited a restaurant not far from his house the night before, but as far as I can determine, he'd only gone to work, the restaurant, and his home in the twenty-four hours before his death."

"So, nothing suspicious there."

"No, but we did find something odd. I've been matching trails to the factory workers here as everyone's been reporting to work. I do have three people unaccounted for. I think at least two of them were female medical personnel responding to the call for help, as their trails retreated and mixed with Lady Blatt's."

I pulled out my notebook, jotting all of this down even as I confirmed it for her. "Likely the case. Her doctor is a woman, and I believe there was a nurse on site as well to help."

"Ah, then yes, that's them. But that leaves one trail I can't account for. It was male, that much I'm sure of."

"And of the right timeline to be involved in the morning explosions?"

"Yes, it coincides perfectly. It could be someone else, though, someone we just haven't accounted for yet."

"Hmm, possibly. Let's keep our eyes open for that. For now, can one of you explain to me why the factory is in use?"

Niamh's face scrunched up in a peeved manner. "I questioned it, too. I didn't want things mixed up with our crime scene. The floor foreman talked to me about it and assured me the offices haven't been touched. He roped them off himself. The rest of the factory was clean, no sign of any disturbance, and apparently they have tough deadlines to meet for their orders. They're very close to shipping out the first batch. Lives will be lost if they shut down, even for a week."

Ahh, snap. Didn't think of that. It was a lifesaving potion, though, literally. For every day they were delayed, it meant people fighting for their lives had less of a chance of recovery. The detective in me mourned the possible loss in evidence. The practical part of me observed we already had the evidence-destruction squad through here anyway so might as well just roll with it.

"Have you been up to the office yet?" I inquired of them.

"Only up to the doorway. We didn't cross the rope," Eddy promised.

"Okay. Well, let's go up. Eddy, you can run me through those possible points of entry when we get back down."

"Sure, sure."

I caught them up as we went in, explaining how Lady Blatt had been found in an interesting position. Not to mention that Celto had also been restrained and the suicide note was bogus. There were personal protection necklaces right inside the door, which I made note of, although not many were hanging there. All the employees would have theirs on, of course. I made sure the two with me wore one, as well as my cats, but I didn't bother. Nothing in this factory could possibly harm me. Everything in here was magic infused, and the spells on me would deflect it without issue. I mean, a vat of potion spilling over me would be unpleasant, but it's not like it would do damage.

The inside of the factory was interesting in its own right. When I thought of old-time factories like this, I always thought of the huge machinery that went from floor to ceiling, churning and cranking along. This didn't quite match that internal vision. It looked more like a giant brewery, really. There were huge vats every dozen feet or so, with some of them red-hot as they cooked. Other pipes extended over the mouth of the vats, pouring in ingredients. I could see another station much further away, along the back wall, that looked like ingredient prep. Really, the place was just a giant kitchen.

A werebear took note of us as we came in and turned, looking me over before approaching with a ground-eating stride. He had foreman written all over him, especially with that fire retardant black jacket and the clipboard in his hand.

He offered a paw in greeting. "Berrycloth. I'm foreman for this floor."

I shook it, carefully. Strong as I was, I wasn't matching strength with a werebear. Seemed like a poor life decision. "Jamie Edwards, Queen's Own. Foreman, I'd love to talk to you, but can I go up and look at ground zero first?"

"Please do, ma'am. I'm not going anywhere. You tell us all how we can help. We're right mad about Lady Blatt. Good woman, and she didn't deserve to be hurt in that way."

Mad about Lady Blatt but not your boss, Celto? Oooh, there were delicious undercurrents here. I was definitely intrigued. "I'm happy to say it looks like she'll survive this."

His furry face lit up in a smile. "Will she?"

"We brought up a royal mage with us to look her over and he was able to boost her healing. Says he'll be surprised if she doesn't wake up on her own accord by midweek."

"Ma'am, I have to tell you, you just made everyone here happy. Best news we've had since this sad business went down."

"I thought it might be. Let me go up, I want to figure out what went on up there. Then I'll come down and ask you far too many questions."

"I'm happy to answer them, every single one."

I gave him a smile and let Niamh lead me up the stairs. Eddy and cats were right on my heels but I tracked them by ear. I didn't trust any of them to not be distracted. Especially if mice were involved.

The main office was one floor up. The stairs led directly to it and one other room, which seemed to be a records room. I peeked at it through the door but it only had one row of file cabinets and a single table in the middle of the room. Expanding as they needed to, eh? I would have. File cabinets would not be fun to lug up those stairs.

The roped-off room—formerly office—was a different story altogether.

Not much was left of the original furniture. A lot of it was burned, just sooty dark remains abandoned on the floor. I could make out the general shape of a desk, two chairs… make that three, there was a third lurking in the corner that had fared better than all the other furnishings. Still beyond redemption, though. A single file cabinet in the far corner had a drawer open, and it leaned against the wall as if needing the support.

If there had been papers on the desk, or files in the cabinet, they were long gone now. No help there. I ducked and slid below the rope, coming to stand inside the room properly, looking it over with not only eyes but nose. The cats weren't the only ones who could pick up on sniffies. I put on magic specs so I could see the lay of the land, my nose wrinkling as I took it all in.

"A lot of magic was thrown around in here," I observed. "Place reeks of it."

Niamh followed me in, also putting on specs. "You said Lady Blatt was found twisted on the ground like she'd been bound and fallen out of a chair?"

"Yes, precisely so. From the blood spatter…I would say she was here."

I stepped carefully around, edging against the wall, eyes trained on the floor as I read the remains of the blood spatter.

"She was closest to the door. I see more blood spatter up against the wall and window, as Celto was in the chair behind the desk."

"That matches what the police report says."

"So it does. Now, Lady Blatt was magically bound. The bindings were removed before she was found."

Eddy hovered in the doorway, eyes glued on me. "So there really was an attacker? It wasn't just Celto being stupid?"

"Oh, there was an attacker. I can confirm that much, at least. Eddy, this is the window you said was nailed shut?"

"Yeah, you can see the nails poking out and they weren't put in very well."

So it wasn't that he'd been in this room when he wasn't supposed to. Good. "How big were the nails?"

"Long. Like, uh…I dunno, I'm not a carpenter. But too long. You can see the ends sticking out on this side. Outside heads are still shiny, too."

Not enough time for them to weather or rust, so a few days at most?

Eddy tacked on, "The ground slopes up in the back, so it's not as much of a jump as you'd think. There's no window on the main floor for this side of the building. It's probably only four feet or so?"

"Ahh, hence the precaution of nailing the window shut. Our attacker didn't want to risk anyone trying to jump for freedom." How disgustingly thorough of him. "I have a few questions here that need answers. We know how people were oriented, what was inflicted against them, but did Lady Blatt come in under her own power and was then bound?"

Niamh didn't hesitate to answer. "Yes. I show her falling to the floor here, just inside the door. She was ambushed when she came in."

I turned a little to follow her pointing finger. "Wow, really, right there? She probably never saw what hit her, then. Rats, I was hoping she'd be a witness when she awoke. Unless he just hit her with binding spells and kept her conscious, we might be out of luck there."

Eddy questioned this, brows scrunched up. "You don't think she was kept awake?"

"Because of how she was oriented on the floor," I explained patiently. "She was splayed in such a way that she was unconscious when she was down. I will bet you anything you care to name she was propped up in a chair, bound to it, and then when the bindings were cut, she fell straight over without once waking up."

"That's...just wrong," Eddy decided, looking perturbed.

"Trust me, I'm not happy about it either. At least the poor woman wasn't terrified out of her mind when a bomb was set off right against her. That's the only silver lining to this." I looked the scene over again, then rubbed at my nose with the back of my hand. It didn't smell nice in here, to say the least. The ozone of magic, of two bombs going off, the scorched scent of flesh and wood—it didn't make for a nice combination in my nose.

I shook it off as best I could and directed everyone. "Ok, peeps, we need to keep a lookout for anything gnarly, like heavy pockets of magic residue. We'll mark them for Henri's perusal later. Right now, I'm looking for three things. First, a sign that anyone else was up here when they shouldn't have been. Second, the patent. I want to make sure that patent is secure. If this was a robbery gone wrong, that would have been the thing to steal."

"Why?" Eddy asked.

Niamh answered this one. "The patent will list out the precise potion and how to make it. It would tell anyone who stole it how to produce the potion, and that's worth a lot of money."

"Ohhh. Got it. I'll look for it."

I trusted our little thief to find it before anyone else, really. He had the best sense of where these things were kept. "Third thing—and this is just me being nitpicky—but I want to know where Celto graduated from. If the man had enemies from home that followed him up here, then I need info on where he was trained and educated. Find his wizard certification. Most magicians will have theirs displayed on a wall somewhere with their license number. But before we dive in, let's take some pictures, gather some blood samples. The crime scene is pretty contaminated, but let's process it best we can. Gloves on, please. Eddy, you stand right there at the door while Niamh and I work. Actually, go next door to the file room and start searching for the patent."

I got nods from both and then we all split. Eddy headed for the file room next door, as that was likely where the patent was. I pulled out my camera and got to work.

"How did the attacker get out?" I asked Niamh as I worked the room.

"From what I can tell, the same way he came in. The door. There's a lot of traffic in and out of this room, so I'll have to parse through the tracks, but there's no sign of anyone going out the window or entering that way."

Made sense, what with the nails in it and all. And that was the only other point of entry. "Any sign of major magic? Portaling spells are a possibility."

"Only heavy signs of magic I see are where the two bombs went off. RM Davenforth might be the better one to answer that question."

"Yup, and I'll ask him, just curious if you saw something I didn't."

Pictures done, I swabbed up some blood samples and labeled them, but there wasn't much left of the room. Just piles of debris. "Niamh, start in on what's around the desk, see if anything interesting survived. I'm going to help Eddy."

"Okay."

Clint and Tasha came with me, both sniffing around. I opened a few files on the table for Clint to comb through.

So someone explain to me why Tasha was the one who actually helped search the files?

I swear to you, Clint had the attention span of a water flea some days.

We were barely at it any time at all when Niamh came to me holding a broken frame in her hand. She'd cleared out the glass, at least, as a precaution before handing it over. "Wizard certification."

I took it and looked it over. Seemed legit. "I don't know the school but no surprise there. I'm not familiar with Itauen. Henri will probably know better than me. Okay, that's one down. Bag and tag, then help us search for a patent."

"One thing first. Eddy?"

Eddy popped up hopefully.

"The bottom drawer of the file cabinet in the office is locked. Can you open it and search there?"

You'd think he'd been given license to be bad. "Sure!"

In a flash, Eddy was back in the office.

Niamh headed for the other side of the cabinets, tackling those. "By the by, he was golden for me while you were at the hospital. I didn't have to worry about him once."

"Good to hear, but I'm not surprised. Eddy doesn't really have a problem with authority. He's just weak against boredom. As long as you give him something interesting to do, he's generally a pretty good kid."

"Is that why you're training him?"

"That, and it's a waste to ignore his natural talent. He's keen to learn and make a career of it. Why not train him?"

"Ahh. I did wonder." Niamh took files to the table before stating, "I'll help you."

I turned sharply to look at her, more than a little surprised by this. Most people wanted to strangle Eddy after about twenty-four hours. Even my patient Henri. "Really?"

"He reminds me of my younger brother. Same irrepressible curiosity and energy." Niamh gave me a reassuring nod. "He and I get along fine."

Was that a heavenly choir that just broke out over my head? Oh, thank any saint, angel, and pink elephants I could name. Someone to help me wrangle that kid. "Please. And thank you."

"I think he'll make a good tracker, too, once I hammer some basics into him."

"Oh, now he'll love that."

"Then I'll start teaching him."

I had the feeling Eddy had just acquired a second big sister. Which was excellent—the kid needed it.

We focused on the files. Not that it seemed to do much good; most of them were order forms. Interesting in its own right. I had an idea of the scale of the operation from these, but there wasn't a patent anywhere in here.

Eddy popped in with Berrycloth in tow, and I didn't like the frown on his face. I stopped mid-flip and eyed him sharply.

"Eddy, that's your Serious Face. What trouble are you bringing to me?"

"Bad news," he said apologetically. "I couldn't find the patent in the other office, so I thought, maybe Mr. Berrycloth would know where it was."

Now that was obvious and why hadn't I asked that?

Berrycloth rumbled out in his deep voice, "It should have been in the top drawer of that file cabinet in Celto's office. That's where he's always kept it, to my knowledge."

"That drawer was pried open." Eddy gestured through the wall to where it sat. "There's no ash in there, either. It didn't get destroyed in the fire. Jamie, you said that if we can't find the patent, this might be a robbery."

I rubbed at my jaw, facts swirling around in my head and forming a very different picture than I'd initially suspected I'd find here. "Yes, I did. Mr. Berrycloth, is there any possibility that the patent would be somewhere else?"

"That file cabinet in his office is the only one that locked. It can't be anywhere else, ma'am."

That rather did answer the question.

Clint was all bristly, bright-eyed interest at my feet. "So really is?"

"Odds are good, bud. Let's finish going through here first. It might have gotten mixed up with some other paperwork and shuffled into the wrong folder. I've seen that happen more than once. But if we can't find it, then the odds are good this is a robbery that went wrong."

It didn't quite sit right with me, though. Staging this like a murder-suicide to cover the thief's tracks made more sense to me now. But using bombs to kill them both? Magical bombs that Henri told me would take some magical expertise?

What kind of a magician would turn thief like this?

Report 09: Local Hero

I arrived at the hotel that evening with a mixed sense of accomplishment. I had determined several things, all of which would help our case, but none of them brought a clear answer as to what exactly had happened. Or even why. Unlike what they show in those dreadful, cheap detective novels, motivation was not always discovered. Sometimes we closed a case without ever truly understanding the perpetrator's drive for the act. That said, we did like motive. It helped solve a case more often than not.

This picture was getting weirder by the second, and I'd like to know just what I was looking at.

Eddy Jameson met me in the dining room with a spring in his step and a wide smile on his face. I trusted this expression not one iota. It normally indicated mischief. I hoped in this case it just meant he'd found something helpful to the case.

"Doctor, Evans, we found things!" Jameson greeted cheerfully. "Well, we didn't find one thing, which we should have, which is the same as finding something."

That logic hurt my brain. "Mr. Jameson, do back up and start from the beginning."

"Start with where Jamie and Niamh are," Evans requested.

"Oh, they're walking the outside of the factory one more time before coming back. Jamie wanted to see where people could enter. There's a few windows without locks, and the main office window—you know, where things went kablooey—that one's nailed shut."

Now that was intriguing information. "From the inside or outside?"

"Outside." His chest puffed up with pride. "Found that one myself. Anyway, Jamie wanted to see how hard it might be to break in there, and Niamh said there was one window on the second floor where it looked like someone had entered, so she's getting a better look at that. I'm cold and starving so they sent me to you."

I exchanged a loaded look with Evans. That painted an interesting picture. I wasn't entirely sure what to make of it just yet, but I wasn't surprised someone had broken in. If we could figure out how they had entered, we might find out who.

I didn't want to discuss this standing right inside the hotel's dining room so hailed a wait staff and requested, "A table for five, please."

"Of course, sir, just a moment." The weredog moved off, presumably to check for a table to seat us. The dining room looked very full. I could hear the chatter of patrons just out of sight, and it was a good sign that this place offered excellent cuisine. I hoped so, as I was quite starved.

Jameson was on a roll and not to be deterred. "First, the thing we didn't find. We didn't find the patent."

He'd had my attention from the start, but I felt my focus on him sharpen. "At all? Where should it have been?"

"File cabinet in his office, according to the floor foreman. But it had been pried open—bad job, too, totally amateur work—and no sign of it anywhere. We checked the other file cabinets just in case but it still wasn't to be found."

Evans made an enlightened rumble. "Sounds like we have some motive. Theft."

I was of two minds on this. "I agree that's a very

sound possible motive, but why kill two people? Or attempt it, at any rate. Silencing witnesses?"

"Could have been that." Evans turned to Jameson. "What else?"

"Jamie found Celto's wizard certification and said she didn't recognize the school. Oh! And Lady Blatt's position on the floor was strange."

Without further prompting, he handed me Tasha and the notebook, and then much like a marionette with its strings cut, flopped promptly onto the ground without care. I winced as he did so. Truly, what was it about teenage boys that they had no regard for personal safety or the possibility of injury? My thirty-plus-year-old self would have feared not only strained muscles but broken bones if I'd attempted such a thing.

I wasn't alone in this, either, as Evans visibly winced alongside me.

Eddy's position was interesting, however, and despite the fact we were in a public place, I held him there for a moment longer. "Truly, just like that?"

"Yuppers. Jamie demonstrated it for us."

How she knew to do so was a question I'd pose to her later. In the meantime, I offered Jameson a hand and levered him up to his feet, which he did with a light bounce as if landing on a tile floor hadn't left so much as a bruise behind.

Youth. I said that with both envy and despair.

"If she was oriented in such a way," Evans murmured to me, "then it looks as if she was bound then fell out of a chair, or tossed inside a room. She may not have been conscious at all when the bombs went off."

"Ambushed at the door," Jameson corrected him. "That's what Niamh said. She said Lady Blatt's body hit the floor right inside the doorway."

Then odds were very much against her seeing her attacker. I muttered several internal curses. I'd truly hoped she would be able to name who had done this. Alas, odds were slim.

The waiter came back and guided us to a table. I was relieved to sit after hours of standing and working. My back especially appreciated not being bent at a forty-five-degree angle over a table.

The atmosphere here was one of comfort, a cozy at-home feeling. In this country, they had blankets attached under the table, with thick padded chairs and a small inset brazier in the middle of the tabletop. All in an effort to combat the chill, I presume, and I appreciated it enormously. Just the short trip from the police station's morgue to our hotel had chilled me right to the bone.

Phil went directly from my coat pocket to my lap, burrowing under the blanket over my legs. He'd grown to such a size that he took up the majority of my lap. I looked down in amusement, not seeing so much as a whisker peeping out.

"Can you breathe?"

"Yes," he mirped back.

Well, as long as he wasn't suffocating under there. I noticed that Tasha had also disappeared and not a moment later felt her maneuver onto my lap as well. She and Phil were curled up tightly together and I had the premonition that until they were warmed, nothing short of a small disaster would encourage them off my lap. Despite them being squished together.

Ah well. At least they were still light and wouldn't cut off all circulation to my legs.

We were at a table in the back of the room, situated relatively near a fireplace, which gave us some privacy from the other diners. Just as well, as I suspected we'd discuss the case at length over dinner.

I took the pad out of my pocket and messaged Jamie.

Where are you?

On our way back. ETA ten minutes.

We're in the dining room. Shall I order for you?

Anything soupy and hot. Niamh says the same for her.

Understood.

The waiter came by with menus and, after a moment of deliberation, I ordered for myself and the ladies. Jameson ordered enough food to feed a small family, but considering how quickly he grew, he likely was starved. I let him be.

Our order was barely placed when a man in a dark suit and anxious smile approached our table. He extended a hand to me, which felt awkward with me sitting, but he stayed me with a hand when I attempted to rise.

"Please don't, Royal Mage, you must be chilled after working all day. Rest. I just wanted to introduce myself. I'm Quill, the owner of the hotel. I learned today who our esteemed guests are and I'm very glad you're here."

"You've been an excellent host to us so far, sir, and we appreciate it. I'm Henri Davenforth. These are my colleagues, Eddy Jameson and Queen's Agent Evans. I'd show you the Felixes but they're consumed with cold and not inclined to come out of the blanket."

"I quite understand, it's been a brisk day even for us natives. I wanted to stop by and tell you that all expenses are paid as long as you're here under my roof."

I blinked up at him in surprise. "I beg pardon?"

"I owe Mister Celto a great deal, you see, and I want to repay that debt as I can. Aiding the people who will solve his murder is the only method I see available to me. I—" He looked away, visibly upset, eyes bright with unshed tears. Strong emotion rippled along his jaw before he could bring himself to speak again. "We're all very upset about this."

Yes, the sincerity of that was obvious. It left me with no few questions, though, as I didn't see an obvious connection between these men.

Evans leaned forward to see around me and ask, "How did you know Celto?"

"When he first came here, touring the area to build a factory and such, he found that there were several cases of consumption here. He was alarmed that this place was infected with the very thing he wanted to cure. He enlisted the help of several local magicians and those of us willing to harvest the necessary ingredients, and set to work immediately. We were his first subjects in Haverford. My mother, father, and younger sister were on the verge of death before he stepped in. His potion cured them. I'd be entirely without family if not for him."

So Celto was a local hero. Oh my. Quill's reaction, then, did make more sense.

"Mister Quill, I promise you, we will do our best to sort this out and find what truly happened." I shook his hand with mine and gave him my best smile.

"Thank you, sir. I'm…" He had to stop and gather himself again. "I'm very upset by what happened, but I understand your team is the best when it comes to investigating. I trust you'll be able to find the culprit and bring them to justice. Please, whatever you wish, it's on the house. If there's any way I can aid you, just let me know."

"I will. Thank you."

Quill squeezed my hand once more before letting go and leaving us. I blew out a low breath and turned back to my colleagues.

"Well." Evans shook his head. "No wonder people are bending over backwards to help us. It's not just the economic boost the factory brought in here."

"Someone really should have mentioned that Celto had personally saved lives here before this point. It sheds rather a different light on things. Could this possibly have been the work of someone upset that their loved one didn't live when others did?"

"Revenge," Evans murmured. "Oldest motive in the book. It could be. We'll look into that possibility."

I saw Jamie from the corner of my eye as she cleared the main dining room's doors. She always walked as if she knew precisely where she was going and nothing would stop her from reaching her destination. I turned to greet her with a smile.

"There you are, dearest."

"Tell me something hot is coming. Niamh and I are both dreaming of guzzling it down."

"We've placed the order."

"Awesomesauce." Jamie ducked down long enough to give me a quick hug around the shoulders before dropping into the chair next to me, rearranging Clint as she did so. He promptly curled under the blanket as well, unabashedly taking over her lap.

Niamh took a seat next to Jameson and asked, "Did you fill them in?"

"I did," Jameson answered promptly.

"Body position, third person at the door, missing patent, certification, nailed window?"

"Yup."

She gave him an approving nod. "Very good. One more thing to note: I think the person who ambushed them circled the building for several days before attacking. I saw his trail all around in the tree line, and his entrance was through a second-story window. I'll swear to this."

"There's only ground security wards on the building," Jamie threw in for our benefit. "Nothing above that, so by entering the second story, he didn't trigger any alarms."

Evans' mouth pursed in a silent whistle. "Smart of him. So he cased the area, got down Celto's habits and schedule, then attacked. Lady Blatt was an unseen factor, as she was only there for a meeting. He might well have panicked and had to rework his plan on the spot because of her appearance."

It did seem to be that way.

My pad rang in my pocket and I fished it out, not at all surprised to see my queen calling. Most likely for an update. I answered the call then set it on the table between Jamie and myself, as there were questions only she could answer.

"Your Majesty, good evening."

"*Davenforth, I'm quite anxious for word of how today went. Have you discovered anything?*"

"Quite a few things, in fact. First, this was not a murder-suicide. The suicide note was quite cleverly faked. There were binding spells put on Celto's arms and legs—"

"Lady Blatt's too," Jamie pitched in.

"And signs that Celto was rendered unconscious and bound. The angle of the explosion indicated that someone else was in control of the spell, as his hands and arms were some of the least damaged. He couldn't have done this without some clever rigging. I doubt that was the case, as it doesn't explain the removed restraints. I didn't find any trace of narcotics in his system; he had a clean bill of health as far as I can determine. I can quite confidently say that he did not take his own life. We are looking at murder, plain and simple. Motive and suspect currently escape us, but we'll track this down, whomever it was."

There was a long sigh. "*I knew I was right to send you all in. You've already discovered far more than the local police did. How is Lady Blatt?*"

Jamie answered, "Much better. Vonderbank and Dr. Ratliff worked a minor miracle there. They've got her under several healing spells, steadied her breathing, and said she will probably wake up on her own by midweek. Maybe even eat."

I blinked at her in astonishment. Truly? "Despite the damage she took?"

She shook a finger at me. "Despite that. I verified she was wearing one of those safety necklaces they have at the factory door. Smart girl to do that. It's what saved her. The necklace charm diverted quite a bit of the force."

"Will she recover, then?"

"Vonderbank says so. Her fiancé absolutely refuses to leave her side until she's ready to go home. I really like the guy, I can see why she fell for him. Oh, Queen Regina, Vonderbank wants to stay up here too until he's sure she's out of the woods."

There was a moment of confused silence. *"Out of the woods...?"*

Jamie growled in amused frustration. "Freakin' translation spell, I swear. I mean, recovered enough for him to be satisfied. He's also put up wards around her room just in case the attacker comes back. I think he's having fun talking to the pretty doctor up here, too. I stopped by on the way back to check on things and he was flirting with her. Did you know Vonderbank could flirt?"

Regina chuckled. *"No, that must be a sight. I'm sorry to have missed it. You've made a great deal of progress in the first day of investigation. I'm pleased. I'll relay all of this to Egon. For now, what do you think the motivation is? Was this professional jealousy, perhaps?"*

"Well, here's the thing. The patent is missing. My vote's on theft and a bad coverup."

I tacked on, "Second possibility is revenge. Celto apparently cured many people when he first arrived, although he had to scramble and draft help to make enough potions to cure the consumption here. If he failed to cure someone's loved one, it's a possibility a family member or lover was out for revenge."

Jamie's *oooh* was twelve syllables long as she dragged it out. "Plot thickens. I didn't know that. How do you know that?"

Evans answered, "Hotel manager stopped by and introduced himself. We have all expenses paid here. He's invested in us solving the case. Said Celto saved three of his family members from sure death."

"Well, well, well." Jamie stared off into space, and I could see that powerful intellect slotting this information into place. "That does spin things in an interesting direction, doesn't it? I don't know if more motives are helpful or not right now. On the one hand, more information, yay! On the other, it might distract us from what we need to actually focus on."

It was a game we played often, almost with every case. "Should we bet on it? I think this was revenge."

"Oh, I'm all for robbery," she countered immediately. "If it was just revenge, the suspect wouldn't have stolen the patent."

Drats, she did raise a good point there.

"Bet all you like," Regina drawled, *"but do remember to keep me updated. If I can aid Lady Blatt or her family, pass along any requests. I do not wish for her and her fiancé to feel isolated up there."*

"Absolutely," Jamie promised.

I had no idea what my queen could possibly do from an entirely different continent, but I also knew better than to question her determination. This woman routinely moved mountains when it was necessary for them to move. All the women of my association were quite formidable.

Which was why I didn't believe for one moment the culprit would get by with this. One way or another, he would be chased down like the monster he was. I quite looked forward to it.

Report 10: Things are Not as They Appeared

There's a saying on Earth: A man's reputation would not know his character if they met on the street.

That's very apt in this case.

Isn't it, though?

Evans and I started our morning at the factory.

Well, really, we all did, but our team was on two entirely different tasks. Jamie, Niamh, and Jameson set themselves to interviewing the workers here. Evans and I wanted to review the potion-making process. Without the patent, we knew very little about how it worked. Something about this might be key to this entire case. It might not. I wouldn't know until later so it behooved me to ask questions now.

Despite it being Gods Day, the factory was in full swing. This didn't surprise me overly much, as they were no doubt trying to make up for lost time. They had deadlines to meet, after all.

It may be blisteringly cold outside, but the inside of the factory was warm indeed. A touch too warm; I might regret the heavy coat I had on by the time I finished this tour. This ground floor was all for cooking—or so it seemed—with vast cauldrons sitting on burners looming on either side of us. It left just enough of a walkway to make our way through without being crowded.

The floor foreman, Berrycloth, greeted us with a pleased smile. "RM Davenforth, Queen's Agent Evans, happy to show you around. You both have protection charms on? Good, good, never hurts to be careful in here. Miss Jamie said you had questions for me."

Of course Jamie had already made friends with him. Of course she had. My extrovert lover didn't know how to do anything else. I did do a mental double-take at being addressed so, as I still wasn't quite accustomed to hearing my new title. "I have many questions for you, sir. I know absolutely nothing about how this potion is made. I understand half the ingredients are native to this area, hence the location of the factory, and that's all I know."

"Well, I can tell you a good bit more than that. First, the ingredients." Berrycloth paused to lean in and murmur, "This is supposed to be a trade secret, but seeing who you are, I can in good conscience tell you."

"I appreciate that, thank you."

He straightened again. "*Rubilium*, specifically the tube, the leaves of *Proscinem*, seeds of *Satviri*, the whole plant of *Totobuit*, leaves of *Terratas*, fruit and seeds of *Britclara*—although that one's imported—"

I was somewhat surprised as *Britclara*, otherwise known as willow fruit, thrived in a much warmer climate than here. It would be native to Parreira.

"—and finally, the roots of *Virigus*."

My understanding of the process ground almost immediately to a halt. Why, one might ask? Well, the answer was simple. I had taken a look at Celto's wizard certification and, quite frankly, he was only a middling wizard.

He absolutely did not have the credentials to take these herbs—some of which could be poisonous if used incorrectly—and know how to combine them into a potion with healing effects.

Something of this must have shown on my face, as Berrycloth gave me a knowing look and nodded.

"You, sir, know your herbs."

Evans looked between us, confusion tightening his brows. "Eh? What?"

"This doesn't make sense to me," I told him, then paused, as I wanted to word this right. "It's...you saw the certification for Celto yesterday."

"Right. He's level one, according to it."

"To someone with no knowledge of magic or herbology, on the surface, he would have the knowledge to put a potion like this together. But that assumes several things. It assumes that he has an inherent understanding of herbology in his native environment."

Evans was a Queen's Own agent for good reason. He immediately cottoned on to the problem. "But half the herbs in this potion are from a different environment than he grew up in."

"Precisely. That's half the problem. The other is that three of these herbs—namely the *Proscinem*, *Totobuit*, and *Virigus*—can be quite deadly if not prepared or dosed correctly. How would he, a man not native to this country, know how to use these? How to balance them out with the other herbs in such a way that it would heal and not kill? With a level one wizard's training? I find my credulity stretched beyond belief."

Evans slowly nodded in understanding, frown growing. "I'm with you on this. That does seem strange. Unless he came up here specifically to study under someone?"

"Why would he do so? Why not use the plants and herbs native to his own country first and foremost? It would be very expensive and time consuming to reach out to other experts to do what he did. This makes less sense the more I look at it."

Berrycloth cleared his throat to draw our attention back to him. "I'm about to muddy the waters even more. I don't think he knew how to use these herbs."

I stared at the werebear and felt my doubts rise even further. "Why do you say so?"

"Let's walk and talk. I'll demonstrate as we go."

Amenable to this, I fell in alongside him as we walked the aisle between the massive cauldrons. I was cautious not to brush up against anything. The heat radiating off them alone warned the passerby. Significant burns would follow to the unwary. The protection charms given to all visitors and workers made more sense as I walked. Not to mention the smell, thick with earth and plants, might well fell someone without the added protections. It was overpowering even through the protective shield.

Berrycloth pointed to the first cauldron to our right. "*Rubilium* there. When we first met him, Celto tried to just cut this thing off with a knife and haul it with a cloth bag."

I winced. I couldn't think of a more amateur move than that.

Evans pointed toward me. "I can tell from his expression that was a stupid thing to do, but one of you explain it to me. I'm not an herbologist."

Berrycloth paused and regarded me quizzically. "Are you? Is that why you were sent up here to investigate?"

"No, sir, quite the contrary. But I started out my career as a magical examiner with the police."

His expression cleared, enlightenment dawning. "Then you do understand more than the average magician about herbs and such. Now it makes sense why you were sent."

"I assure you, my better half is the main reason. Jamie is the investigator of the two of us. But let me explain this to Evans. In short, you don't want to disturb the tube of the plant until you need it. The juices held within the tube are what is actually potent and what you need to harvest. Also, anything made of cloth would absorb the juices and render the rest of the plant practically useless before it could be used."

Evans was back to being confused. "Wait, so he didn't even understand that, but he somehow knew how to properly use this herb in a very complex potion?"

"You understand why Berrycloth and I winced now, don't you?"

"I'll say. Continue, please."

Berrycloth did so. "Second problem is this vat to the left. We put in several protective wards around the top of it, then vented it outside through the stacks, and I had to argue with Celto about doing both. He kept maintaining that it just added to the expense, that there was no need for it. Man didn't even know that the *Totobuit's* leaves will give off a deadly gas when boiled. How he was ignorant of that was my main question because you can't even harvest these things in the rain. One strong rainstorm or careless breath in and you don't wake up the next day."

I rubbed at my forehead, already feeling a headache coming on. "Great dark magic, I don't like how this is adding up."

Evans growled out a curse. "This man...some are claiming he's a hero. Others claimed he's brilliant. But right now, you're describing him as an idiot."

"Sirs, I'll be frank. I think he was a fraudster." Berrycloth waved a hand around to indicate the factory as a whole. "I don't know where he got this potion from. I just know he couldn't possibly be the creator of it. He didn't know enough about herbology to make it. He barely knew where the plants were coming from. I didn't realize how ignorant he was until we got in here and started putting together the equipment needed to brew. I'd worked in potion factories before, for a good fifteen years. I know the difference between a good boss and a bad boss. Celto was not a good boss."

Evans pushed the question I didn't quite dare say aloud. "If you knew he couldn't possibly have created this potion, why still work for him? Why not report him?"

"Two reasons. One, I had no proof of it. It's only my own observations and opinions—what could I possibly tell a policeman of this? They wouldn't have enough knowledge of magic and herbs to understand what the problem was."

That was a valid point all on its own. Indeed, what policeman would know enough to be able to understand the problem? Evans was a powerful magician in his own right and still had to have some things explained to him.

"Second—and this sounds greedy of me—I cared less about who created it and more that it was distributed. The world needs this potion. Sometimes we have thousands of deaths in a single year because there's nothing to cure consumption. I couldn't…" Berrycloth trailed off, eyes sad. "I just couldn't jeopardize the whole operation based on my suspicions. However he came about the formula, it worked. It could save hundreds of thousands of lives. Who was I to stop that from happening?"

Also a valid reason. I put a hand on his shoulder. "Sir, I can't fault you for it. In your position, I may well have made the same decision. Thank you for your honesty. This does raise other questions and sheds light on the case in a way that might help us solve it."

His relief was palpable. "Thank you for not judging me harshly. I've lost many a night of sleep over this. I've second-guessed my decision to keep quiet many times."

"Don't beat yourself up anymore," Evans advised. "I'm with Davenforth on this. You did the best you could with a bad situation. I'm suddenly quite glad you gave us this tour. We really learned things we needed to. Can you complete it? I want to understand this full process before we go back to Jamie and Niamh with an update."

"Of course, sir, of course. We've got this crushing station next, with the leaves of *Proscinem*. Its properties are for the lungs, to counter the cough that comes with consumption."

I let him walk, lending half my attention to him,

but my mind mostly fixated on something else entirely.

Quill had told me in passing that when Celto first arrived in country and saw the situation for what it was, he had hired local magicians and such to help him create the potion necessary to immediately tend to those suffering from consumption. At the time, I hadn't thought anything of it. Depending on the number of patients, it only made sense to hire help. One man could only brew so many potions in a day, after all. Especially if he needed to harvest the necessary ingredients, then he likely couldn't have done more than a dozen potions at a time with an at-home workstation.

But what if that wasn't the reason Celto had hired help? What if he knew that he didn't have the necessary skills in order to brew anything? The more I walked this path with Berrycloth, the more apparent it became how complex this potion was. Anything over three ingredients in a potion required considerable skill. Here he had seven. Seven! And different parts of seven, no less, everything from the seeds of one plant to the entirety of another.

Brewing a batch of a potion was one thing, creating a large quantity of it in a factory setting another entirely. It was the difference between making a single pudding or making a batch of it for commercial consumption. The quantity of the ingredients wasn't the only thing that changed. Cook times, chill times, all of that changed as well. It took a skilled and knowledgeable person to know how to adapt a singular recipe into something made for commercial use.

I had a feeling Berrycloth or his colleagues had done that work, too. If Celto didn't even know how to properly harvest the herbs of this area, then he certainly didn't know enough to adapt a potion formula to cook in large quantities like this.

If Celto didn't have the knowledge, the training, to create this potion, then where did it come from? Was this something he'd acquired with full permission from the creator? Or had he stolen it? Had he died because he'd stolen the potion formula and the creator had come to wrest it back?

Was the motive revenge after all?

Whatever the case, I did not look forward to telling my queen that she had invested in a fraudster.

> Yeah...that's not going to go over well.

Why don't you tell her.

> Freaking no way. Hard pass. You tell her.

I don't want to tell her. Get her drunk first at a Girls' Night and then tell her.

> Like we have time for me to go back and get her drunk first. Rock, paper, scissors?

We could just play Sails...but fine. Best out of three.

Report 11: Identity Theft is Not a Joke, Jim

I sat next to Niamh as we rode back down into the town. The factory interviews had been interesting. Every worker there had the same thing to say about Celto: nice enough man but clueless about herbology. Every. Single. Person.

Now, wasn't that curious and strange?

Niamh had her head glued to the window of the taxi, tracking from here. She'd run out of daylight yesterday before we could follow the trail of the stalker from the factory and down into the town again. Since the interviews had taken a few hours, we had plenty of time to chase down this lead, and chase we did.

Eddy sat across from us, a lap full of cats and many a question on his lips. "Jamie, is it possible for someone to make a potion and not know how to make big batches of it?"

"Yeah, it kinda is. Henri would do a better job explaining this, but it's like…" I trailed off, trying to think of a good example. "It's kind of a different specialty. I have a recipe, for instance, that try as I might, I can't double it. It never tastes right. Something about the chemistry of the ingredients just don't work in different proportions. It's why experts are called in for this kind of stuff. That said, if Celto really was intelligent enough to have concocted this potion, he shouldn't have struggled so much to do anything at the factory. He'd at least have been consulted with and been able to help the process along."

Eddy nodded thoughtfully, making a light growling sound in his throat. "I thought it strange too. If I asked Henri for a potion, he could make me one. Because he's that smart.

I don't think Celto was smart."

"You're correct," Niamh chimed in, her eyes still on the road. "I think Celto got his hands on that potion somehow. He wasn't the creator. He was just very charming and good at hoodwinking people."

"He was also good at picking personnel, apparently, as he hired all the right people to cover up his multitude of sins." I tapped my pencil to my bottom lip for a moment before making a note of something to follow up on. Just who had vetted this man's credentials? Anyone? Or had they let the potion do the talking for Celto? I had a feeling it was that.

"I betcha he got bombed because he stole something and the creator wanted revenge." Eddy nodded sagely. "I betcha that's it."

"You might well be right. We can't assume that just yet, though. Niamh, how's the trail?"

"Still strong. He definitely came this way." She flicked her apple-green eyes to me. "I suspect he went straight to the docks and onto a boat from the factory."

"I sure would have, in his shoes. Why stay and bring suspicion down on yourself? He had what he wanted, anyway. Might as well leave while the leaving was good."

We reached the base of the slope and onto the relatively flat section of city road. I phrased it so because nothing in this place was really flat. All the roads had either a slight rise or a slight descent. Part and parcel of being near a mountain range, I supposed.

Our taxi driver was one of those who wanted to help with the case, so he was very amenable to taking direction instead of delivering us to a fixed address. He'd also been unabashedly listening in this whole time. One of his ears had been swiveled and trained on us as we spoke. Couldn't fault him there; I'd be just as curious. Weredog that he was, he still had a jacket on despite all the fur, which told me I wasn't being a wimp when it came to the cold.

"Queen's Own, which way?" he called over his shoulder.

"Keep heading for the docks, please."

"Sure, sure." He took a slight turn as the road curved, the wheels bouncing over a rut in the road. "Say, I've heard you talking. So that rumor was true?"

I leaned forward a little. "What rumor?"

"Heard the factory workers a time or three at the pub, talking about how Celto didn't know how to run anything. How they had to work overtime to redo something because he couldn't be relied on. No one was happy working for him but they wanted the cure, didn't they? They wanted that cure out in the world, so they stuck with it. So that rumor was true? It wasn't just them blowing off steam over a bad boss?"

"Seems like the rumor had some truth to it, yes. You're the first person I've heard say something about the rumor."

"Well, it was all pub talk, wasn't it? No one put much stock in it, I don't think."

Fair enough. Men with alcohol in their system were never really taken seriously.

Niamh directed us toward the docks with unerring accuracy and we all got out. Our taxi driver agreed to wait, as this wouldn't take more than a few minutes. Niamh could hardly follow a trail over water, after all. I went looking for the port master. Someone here must keep track of what ships came and went.

A small brick office, painted white with a green roof, sat squarely at the edge of the docks. I couldn't read this country's native language, but I saw people coming in and out with clipboards in their hands, so it looked promising. I headed straight for it and poked my head in.

It was small, with four desks shoved inside and file cabinets between them. Clean, though, and with a fresh pot of tea brewing on a little potbelly stove. An aging man with a portly stomach and thick white mustache greeted me with a smile.

"Oh, hello, can I help you?"

I flipped my badge up for him to see it. "I'm Jamie Edwards, Queen's Own from Kingston. I'm—"

"The one investigating the murder, aren't you? Pleasure,

ma'am, pleasure. I'm Elton, Port Master. Tell me how I can help you."

I seriously loved how everyone was willing to help. Made my life so much easier. "Mister Elton, we've tracked someone suspicious down to your docks. The one just outside this building, to be precise. Can you tell me what ships left the day of the attack?"

"I absolutely can, one moment. You said dock eight?" He immediately got up and headed for a large book sitting on another desk. Seriously, this thing was epic grimoire tome in size. I wouldn't be surprised if it held the secret of the universe. Elton flipped through it quickly, going back several pages, then grunted in satisfaction.

"Three left that day, in fact. The first one was early in the morning, about ten o'clock it shoved off. The *Zephyr*. It headed for Itauen. Passenger ship, that one, although it had some cargo too."

I jotted this down hastily. Oooh, I liked that timing. It made the ship a good possibility. Also, the connection to Itauen made my mental tail wag. Celto had been schooled there, so the possibility of trouble following him from that country was strong.

"Second ship was much later in the day, midafternoon. The *Wanderlust*. It came and docked just long enough to let off several passengers before retreating and— Oh, sorry, it didn't leave that day. It stayed in harbor for a day, due to needing repairs to its main mast."

"Ah. So likely not a good candidate."

"No indeed. Third ship also arrived at dock eight and didn't depart again until the next morning. The *Slanderous Puppy*."

I blinked at the name. "Get out. They did not name a ship that."

Elton chuckled, his belly shaking. "Not the strangest name I've seen for a ship, ma'am. Not by any stretch."

"I can believe that. Sailors have a strange sense of humor sometimes. Well, looks like I really only have one possibility."

"You sure it was dock eight? I had other departures on that day."

"Let's step outside and ask my tracker."

I retreated outside, wincing as the wind cut right through my coat, making my bones rattle.

Niamh and Eddy weren't far. They came up to meet me without prompting.

"Did he go anywhere else?" I asked her.

"No, he boarded a ship right from that dock. His trail ends there." Niamh perked up. "You have a name?"

"Only one ship left that day. Two others were here, but they stayed in harbor for a night before leaving. I doubt it's them. The one that left was bound for Itauen."

"Ooooooh," Eddy intoned, eyebrows doing some ridiculous waggling. "Plot thickens!"

This kid had been hanging around me too long. Clearly. "That it does. Mister Elton, that was very helpful, thank you so much. Can I possibly get a ship's manifest of who left?"

"I'd have to reach out to someone else to get it for you, but I think I can manage. It'll just take a day or two."

"Excellent, please do. We're at that hotel there on the corner."

"Oh, Quill's place? Sure, I'll leave it at the desk for you."

Figured he'd know the owner. It wasn't that big of a town. "Thanks so much. I really appreciate it."

Elton leaned in and whispered, "You think that was our killer, then?"

I leaned in to whisper back, "I don't know. At the very least, he may be a witness. I'd really like to talk to him either way."

He gave me a knowing nod. "I would. I'll get you that manifest."

"Thanks. Come see me at the bar sometime and I'll buy you a round." I waved and herded people back into the taxi.

Our taxi driver was even more eager than we for the next destination. His tongue kept sneaking out the side of his mouth in a happy pant. Something about being on the trail of a suspect made his weredog hunting instincts happy, was my guess.

"Where to next?"

I climbed in and directed, "Do you know which hotel Lady Blatt was staying at?"

"I do. There?"

"There." I understood the room had been preserved without cleaning. I wanted to take a look at it, just to see if there were signs of something off. You never knew with people sometimes.

The hotel in question wasn't far, just around the corner and up a block, in fact. Our taxi once again waited while we went in.

The staff was helpful like everyone else and showed me the room in question.

The room, however, was not helpful.

It was a fancy hotel room, nothing more. White bedding, clothes in the armoire, bathroom with some bottles of lotions and makeup and toiletries, as one would expect. It barely looked as if she'd slept here.

Niamh prowled around the room, checking the window and such, before coming back to me with a shrug.

"Two people in here. The employee that let us in and Lady Blatt. No sign of anyone else."

Again, not helpful. Well, it was in the sense of process of elimination. I turned to the employee and asked, "Lady Blatt arrived when?"

"Late in the day, miss. She came in, dined, then came up to her room to rest. I served her breakfast here the next morning, as she was in a hurry to get to the factory before it started up for the day. We chatted a bit. She was very excited by how well things were going." The kobold's face drew into an unhappy frown. "Poor dear. I wished I'd delayed her now, somehow."

"Did she travel alone?"

"She did, which was unusual for her."

"You've seen her often, then?"

"Yes, Agent, almost every time she's been here. Her servant came down ill right before she left, and her fiancé couldn't make it. She chose to just come up alone. She said she wasn't going to be here any time at all. She was set to sail back the very morning she was attacked."

So an overnight trip. Odd for aristocracy to go anywhere alone, but her fiancé described her as independent, so this might not be out of character for her.

I didn't have anything else to ask here. Nothing was out of place, so I thanked her for the time and asked if she would pack everything up and store it for now. No reason to keep the room in stasis like this.

We were back at the taxi in twenty minutes.

The taxi driver was definitely curious, as he asked, "Where to next?"

"Do you know where Celto lived?"

"Sure thing. He had an apartment near the market district."

"There, please."

It was again a very short ride, barely fifteen minutes. The apartment in question was more a townhouse, connected to two others with shared walls, with a small little garden of evergreen bushes out front. This time, the driver got out with us, explaining as he walked.

"I know the owner. She lives in the middle. She'll have a key for you. Missus Dalton!"

It took a moment for the door to open and reveal an aging grandmother with at least three shawls around her neck. She peered up at him and then grunted.

"Ah, hello there. Oh, who's with you?"

"Detectives up from Kingston," he explained, gesturing toward us. "For Celto's murder, you know. Can you let them into his apartment?"

"Gladly. Crying shame what happened to that man. It upsets me, it does."

I leaned around the taxi driver to ask, "Did you know him well?"

"Not well. Always a kind word he had for me when I did see him. Sometimes he brought things up from the market for me, on account of my bad knees. Always paid rent on time, sometimes early. A quiet man. I rarely saw him with visitors." Her blue eyes sharpened on me. "And not once with a lady friend, mark that."

I just loved how everyone was defending Celto's virtue. Or was it Lady Blatt's? Not sure at this point. "Understood, ma'am. If you could let us in?"

She did so promptly, using a giant key ring with enough keys to make her a high school janitor. No kidding.

The townhouse's main floor was an open concept living room and kitchen, all of it whitewashed with light wood furniture and lots of thick, warm textiles. A cozy sort of place. I went through it with gloves on, Tasha and Clint moving ahead of me, their noses going a mile a minute.

Niamh scouted around as well. Eddy seemed engrossed with the shelves and all the books on them. Color me surprised there.

Ms. Dalton and the taxi driver chatted outside while we went through the place. It was clean—surprisingly so for a bachelor—with not much sign of really being lived in. I had a feeling he came here to sleep and not much else. The books and his clothes were the only personal items I saw.

What was more interesting to me was what I didn't see.

I turned to find Eddy right behind me. It was a good teaching moment, so I used it. "Alright, Eddy, what do you think of this place?"

He gave a shrug. "Nice enough. Too easy to break into. I don't think he spent a lot of time here. There's clothes, and books, and he liked to sit in that chair near the fireplace because that's where all the throw blankets are."

Good observation there. "What else?"

"Nothing else here. Don't see no sign of lady friends, the landlady's right there."

"You're correct, I don't see signs of a girlfriend. You know what else I don't see signs of?"

His brown eyes sharpened on me. "What did I miss?"

"You missed what's missing. Think, Eddy. What would Henri's apartment look like? Or Sherard's?"

He turned in place, taking everything in once again, then snapped his fingers. "Where's the magic stuff?"

"Exactly. This man's supposedly a genius wizard but there's nothing here of magic. No herbs, wands, charms, nothing. Henri's relatively neat and still there's things everywhere in his apartment and office that speak of magic."

Niamh came down the stairs from the bedroom to join in. "I'll tell you what else is missing. Visitors. No one has been in here."

That rather put paid to the theory of him having an affair with Lady Blatt, in my opinion. They wouldn't have been able to go anywhere else in this town without getting spotted and remarked on. Not even here was safe, frankly.

Sometimes, what's missing is what's the most important. This place was filled with missing things, if that made sense.

And it was very, very telling.

Report 12: Your Mission, Should You Choose to Accept It

Jamie, no. yes! No. YES! No, why? Henri, yes!

cackles

I sat down with my notebook, my cats, and Eddy to have a pre-dinner meeting. Our amazing host put us into one of his private dining rooms so we had the space to catch up with each other.

It was a rare moment where I had Eddy without anyone around, and I decided to capitalize on it. "Eddy, how goes your studying?"

"Real life or textbook?"

I supposed that was a fair question considering the past few days. "Both."

"Real life, learning all the things." He perked up visibly, that excited light shining in his expression as he connected with something he obviously loved doing. "Niamh's been teaching me how to track, you know, and she set me on someone's trail this morning. It wasn't until they got into a car that I lost them. She said for human eyes, that was really good."

Of course he was good at tracking someone. Of course he was. I swear to any god listening this kid was a natural spy in the making. That's why I started training him to begin with, granted, but it was nice he was picking up the skills quickly.

"Good," I said. I also had to resist the urge to pat his head because he looked like a golden retriever in that moment, but I digressed. "Alright, I want you to continue learning from her. You'll never be quite as good as a Woodland Elf—their eyes are a whole other level—but the more you can learn from her, the better. While you're learning that, I have a new challenge for you."

Eddy loved challenges. Lived and breathed them. The only thing he loved more than a challenge was a new book. Kid practically vibrated in his chair.

"This is worth ten books of your choosing." I arched an eyebrow, judged the bait had been properly set, and bit down on a smile. Careful, Jamie, your evil might be showing. "It's time to hone some pickpocketing skills."

Eddy was absolutely not deterred, just intrigued. "Spies do that?"

"Spies have to acquire information no matter what. The more skills you have in your arsenal, the better. If your mark has secret papers in his pocket, wouldn't it be easier to just slip those out and run away than do some elaborate scheme that might fail?"

Eddy nodded seriously. Well, he was trying to look serious, but he was downright giddy with the idea he could pickpocket people and get away with it.

I knew how he rolled.

"I'll teach you what basics I know—which isn't a lot, I have to warn you—and get you a proper teacher for this when we're back home. There's many a reformed thief who will be happy to teach you the trade for the amount of money I'll pay them. In the meantime, after I teach you some basics, I want you to practice on Evans. Anything you can steal off Evans and bring back to me is proof you've won a round and I'll buy you the books."

Eddy nodded happily, even as he objected, "Not Henri too?"

"Dude, if you can't steal from Henri, then we've got bigger issues. His one-year-old nephew pickpocketed him and he didn't even realize it until his sister called him at work."

Eddy's eyes grew wide, evil delight lifting his mouth up. "Nooo. Did that really happen?"

"It really, truly did."

Eddy cackled. Outright cackled like the Wicked Witch of the West. I think he liked that Henri was not as put together as the man initially appeared.

The door to the dining room opened and both Evans and Henri appeared, taking us in: me balancing two cats on my thighs, Eddy listing sideways in his chair as he laughed.

Henri pointed a finger at him. "Has he finally cracked?"

"I told him how you can literally be robbed by a baby," I answered mock-sweetly.

"Jamie," he growled, exasperated. "Must you repeat that story?"

"Yes. It's too funny to let you live down. Where's Niamh?"

"Right behind us."

People got settled around the table, a waiter came in to take our order, and we situated ourselves enough to work. Even Eddy got ahold of himself, although snickers escaped now and again. Henri absolutely ignored him.

I started us off. "Right, so, I think we can all agree this was definitely murder, although motive is a bit murky right now. There's just too much evidence pointing that direction. We have a third person in that room either right before, during, or after the explosions whom Niamh tracked right to the docks. I have the name of the ship that left at that time, bound for Itauen. I should have the ship's manifest hopefully tomorrow. There's no sign that Celto and Lady Blatt mixed socially."

Niamh picked this up smoothly. "Lady Blatt's hotel room was slept in, nothing more, and she chatted with an employee over breakfast. No sign of a man there with her. Celto's apartment looked barely lived in to us and certainly had no sign of a lady friend there, either. In a town this small, with those two being so famous and known, I don't think they could have gone anywhere together without someone noting it."

Evans grunted in agreement. "I concur. As it is, we're the ones stopped often by people because they know we're working this case. Visitors are rare here so people note them. If there was an affair going on between those two, I think we'd have found some sign of it. I do think Celto might have been up to something nefarious, but I fear Lady Blatt was just in the wrong place at the wrong time."

I had to agree with that assessment, but part of what he said hinted that he knew fun things. I liked fun things. "What did you find to make you think Celto was up to something?"

"From all signs, Celto did not have the knowledge or credentials to make that potion."

I wasn't wholly surprised by this but still very interested in why he said that. "You know, the factory workers all said something about that in my interviews with them. About how much they had to change behind Celto's back because he gave the wrong orders. They were doing a lot of work behind the scenes to get that factory and greenhouse up and running and stopped going to Celto for instructions because it was obvious to them that he didn't actually know what to say. You found the same?"

Henri took up the thread smoothly. "We did. Our tour with Berrycloth and the second-floor foreman was illuminating, to say the least. It's not that Celto lacked the knowledge of how to scale the potion to factory production. That I could understand, as it's rather a tricky problem for those uninitiated to the process. It's that he lacked basic herbology knowledge altogether. For instance, he didn't know how to harvest the *Rubilium* properly; he tried to cut the plant free and put it into a cloth bag. Doing so ruins your efforts of harvesting it entirely. That's just an example. In fact, Berrycloth assured us Celto didn't have a clue how to either harvest or treat any of the herbs correctly without endangering the brewer."

I whistled low. Now, that was telling. Henri wasn't an herbology expert—there's plenty he didn't know—but I could tell from the way he reported this that even he knew better. It told me there was a level of skill, of knowledge, that Celto just didn't have. Then again, he was a level one wizard, so it made sense? Him brewing up a potion that the rest of the world hadn't already concocted, that's what didn't make sense to me.

Apparently, it no longer made sense to anyone at this table.

"One of the things that stood out to us in Celto's apartment was the lack of anything magical," Niamh commented. "There were no magical books or potion-making supplies, barely even any charms. It struck us as odd."

"As it should," Henri answered with a dip of his head. "Even a hedge wizard, for instance, will have all manner of tools of the trade around the house. It's like expecting an engineer to have no wires or gadgets, or an author to have no pen and paper about. Our occupations are part of our lives. It's very strange to see nothing of that in his own personal quarters. I'll put this forward to you: I don't think Celto was the genius people perceived him to be. I think he found that potion somewhere. Or stole it."

I lifted a hand. "I'm for stealing. It makes too much sense. Of course the real creator would want it back. Of course they'd be mad he was about to get filthy rich off of something *they* invented. The attack, the missing patent, a lot is explained if Celto stole the potion."

Evans leaned back in his chair, hands crossed comfortably over his stomach. "I'm for this theory. It also makes sense, then, why the person who was in that office with them retreated to Itauen. After all, Celto's from there. At least one of the herbs used in the potion is from there. I would say odds are, the original creator of the potion is from there as well. Celto didn't come to this country until he had that potion in hand. Ergo, he must have taken it while still living in Itauen."

"I have a feeling the story he concocted about keeping the costs down by being near the source of most of the herbs was just that—a convenient story. If he was to get by with his theft, immigrating to another country was the safest bet." My lip curled up in disgust. I really didn't like thieves. Laziness and envy, that's all theft amounted to.

"You said you're waiting on a ship's manifest?" Evans double-checked. "In that case, after we have a list of names, can we hop back on the yacht ourselves and head over to Itauen? I think our next lead will come from there."

I shared a glance with Henri, got a nod. "I have to agree. I think we've tapped out people to ask questions of and places to investigate here. I keep hoping Lady Blatt will wake up and tell us who the culprit is, but that's likely wishful thinking if she was ambushed from behind."

The door to the dining room opened again. It wasn't food, as I half-expected, but Vonderbank. He looked insufferably pleased with himself, which heralded good news.

"Ah, there you all are. How goes the case?"

"We've ruled out what it can't be and suspect what it might be, so rather well." I gestured him into an empty chair. "We're awaiting dinner if you want to join us."

"Splendid, I think I will. I come bearing good news."

Henri sat up a little straighter. "Lady Blatt?"

"Indeed. I've dared to do a few more healing boosts. Her body type is one that absorbs such magic well, and she's recovered even more. Her lungs have restored independent function, in fact, and her color has improved significantly. I dare say she might not only wake up in a few days, but be well enough to travel home in the next three weeks or so."

Freaking awesome. Seriously, what magic could do. On Earth, a patient like that would be in recovery for months before even a suggestion of going home. Not days. I'd give Vonderbank a high five if the man understood the gesture.

Henri extended a hand and shook Vonderbank's with a wide smile. "Good show, sir. Good show! I hope you've updated Queen Regina. She's hungry for such updates."

"On the way here," Vonderbank assured him. He looked a little too pleased with himself, but he also had cause. "I'm quite delighted that she took a turn for the better. When I first heard of her case, I feared only a grim outcome. Truly, if not for the excellent care she had here, it might have turned out that way. I think I'll stay a few days regardless. I wish to see her awake at the very least before I think of going home."

I couldn't help but tease. "A certain pretty doctor wouldn't have anything to do with that, would it?"

Primly, he retorted, "Dr. Ratliff is an excellent physician who offers scintillating conversation. I find it mentally stimulating to be in her presence."

"Uh-huh. Pull the other foot, man, it has bells on."

He tacked on in that same tone, "She's also agreed to have dinner with me tomorrow night and I shan't pass on such an excellent opportunity."

I slapped a hand lightly to the table as a laugh burst free. "You asked her out? Really?"

Vonderbank's eyes twinkled outrageously. "When one finds a woman of that caliber, one does not foolishly let the opportunity slip past. Where else am I to find a woman that intelligent, beautiful, and capable?"

Henri promptly pointed to me. "Right here."

This smooth talker. I'd reward him for that later.

"Who's not already taken," Vonderbank tacked on dryly. "I shudder to think of what you'd do to me, Davenforth, if I dared flirt with your lady."

"If there was anything left of you after she was done," Henri returned, "I promise you I would invent several curses on the spot. But we digress, I think. We've a lead that will take us into Itauen for several days. On the one hand, I want to speak with Lady Blatt when she's awake. On the other, I do not want this lead to grow cold."

Vonderbank lifted a staying hand. "Let me assure you, I think it better to go chase that lead. Even if I'm right and she awakens soon, she'll be in no condition to speak. Maybe next week, but certainly not this one. She'll be too weak and disoriented with pain to be able to string three words together."

That was fair enough. Her seeing anything was in question, too, so why linger for only a possibility? I'd talk to her regardless, of course, but I had a lead to chase down first.

"Then let's get on the yacht as soon as we have that manifest. Vonderbank, can I entrust this place to you while we're gone? If anything happens, report back to us immediately."

"That I will." Vonderbank paused, head cocked as he studied me. "Do you think something else will happen?"

"No," I answered truthfully. "No, I think our attacker got what he came for—it's why he's gone already—but it never hurts to be careful. I don't want him doubling back because he heard Lady Blatt lived and trying to finish the job. He tried to silence her in the first place because she was a witness. It's on our heads if anything happens to her now."

"Ah. True enough. In that case, I will guard her personally."

"Thanks." I hoped the precaution wasn't necessary, but anyone ruthless enough to put bombs against a living person's torso was more than a little cray-cray and not to be trusted.

At least, I didn't trust them. Not one iota.

Jamie's Additional Report: 12.5

Henri was keen on checking out the greenhouse, and I wasn't ready to turn in yet, so we went back up to the factory for a nightly stroll through the plants. Really, it was nice to have some one-on-one time with him no matter the activity. I strolled along at his side as he paused here and there to bend down and look at some kind of detail on a plant that escaped me.

Just because my eyesight was enhanced and better than a human's didn't mean I understood what I was looking at.

"Is this going to be our backyard?" I inquired of him. "After we get married and settle into a house together, I mean. Will it be overtaken by a massive greenhouse filled with all the plants?"

"Don't be silly," he returned primly. "I'm not a gardener."

That tone was not exactly one of disagreement. I could see the wheels turning from here. "But you want a small one."

"Well, a small one would be practical."

Uh-huh. Called it. "And what would you put in this practical greenhouse?"

"Well, herbs good for common remedies. For colds, or burns, things of that ilk. Certain plants aid in air purification and would be good to have about the house."

I eyed him sideways. I'm on to you, bub. Don't think I was fooled. "You already have a list and a plan for this, don't you?"

"Not a physical list."

"A mental one, then."

"Just an idea," he countered mildly.

These super-brains, I tell you. You had to watch them. You think they're just minding their own business, tinkering with things, but in reality they're making all the plans. They only looked innocent on the surface. "Just remember while you're designing all of this out in your head that I need exercise space and the cats need sunny perches."

"Don't worry, I've accounted for it."

See? He'd been busy thinking about this while I wasn't paying attention. "Your parents must have had a fun time raising you. You always look so innocent, like you're not plotting things, and then the second no one's watching, you get into stuff."

He just snickered. No denial there, huh?

We reached the end of the row and he surveyed the place with a satisfied smile. "They maintain this very well. The plants are thriving. I'll report this to Queen Regina. It should make her marginally happier that even in Celto's absence, things are running smoothly."

"It didn't really matter if he was here or not. He didn't know what he was doing."

"True enough, but reassurances are called for, I think."

"Can't argue that."

He turned to lead us back out, his hand finding mine. "Dessert?"

"Oooh, you do come up with the best ideas."

"I try."

I had to poke him in the ribs. Just because he was being smug.

Clint reports that Eddy was looking for our case notes by the way

Why is your problem child so insatiably curious?

I would love to argue he's not mine but alas…and I dunno. Nature?

He'll be in for a rude awakening.
I have them under locking spells.

You realize you just made them even more tempting, right? lol

He may have gotten past the palace wards, but he won't get past MINE.

yup game is on

Henri's Secret Report: 139

I waited until later that night, when I had the privacy of my hotel room, to call upon Seaton. I wanted a second opinion and, since he knew Jamie as well as I did, I couldn't think of a better person to ask.

He answered promptly, voice high with excitement. *"Finally, you call with an update!"*

"I am not, actually. I'm calling for advice."

"Advice on how to give me an update?"

"Seaton, do focus. I want to propose to Jamie but can't quite settle on a plan."

His tone did an abrupt change, now sounding pleased. *"So the wait is over, eh?"*

"Really, I would have proposed before this if she hadn't been neck-deep in organizing a new department. I still want to wait until after the department officially opens. She's a bit stressed about that, no need to throw something else at her to juggle."

"But you want to plan it out now. I think that's smart."

"I do try," I drawled with a snort. "Now, there's two questions I have no answers for."

"I might not know either, but fire away."

"First, do you know her ring size?"

There was a long pause.

"I take that as a no."

"I've never had occasion to remark on it. I will bet you Ellie Warner would know, though."

"Really? Why?"

"They were inventing something or other that required

measuring Jamie's hands."

"Ah. I'll ask her, then. Now, I'm inclined to do a private proposal that's somewhere scenic and without a crowd."

"*Beach,*" Seaton said promptly. "*Picnic on a beach, or something of that nature.*"

I saw sense in the suggestion the moment he said it. Jamie loved the water and any excuse to be in it was taken with enthusiasm. She'd latch on to the idea of lounging on the beach without any hesitation or questioning of my motives.

"Excellent. I'll plan for that. By the time she's opened the department, the weather will have warmed enough to go to the beach."

"*I hope you've considered, too, the style of ring she wants?*"

The way he questioned this raised immediate alarms. "Why? Is there something I need to know?"

"*Settle in, my friend. This will take a minute. And maybe a few drawings.*"

Oh dear.

Report 13: Celto is Sus

Itauen reminded me of Spain somehow, maybe Italy? It had that kind of European energy and look. The port city we landed in had ships of all sizes docking in the harbor, some of the docks stretching out further than I thought prudent. The land rose abruptly from the shoreline, so that there was only a street with buildings and then foothills jutting out from behind them. The place teemed with sounds, all carried on the wind to my ears, and the air was thick with spices. If Italy married the West Indies and had a baby, I had just met the baby.

For all that Henri was not a social person, he had traveled quite a bit in his life, and it showed in moments like these. He had us all off the yacht, checked out with the ship captain, and into a port hotel in record time. Even as he led me through the doors, he explained over one shoulder how he'd stayed in this particular hotel before and the chefs here knew what they were about. Trust my foodie to remember the place because of the cuisine.

In under two hours we were settled into a hotel. I didn't have the heart to drag everyone back out again—especially Niamh, who struggled with being seasick to begin with. I let them put their feet up or go explore, as their hearts dictated. Henri and I tackled going to the school.

This place didn't know what flat ground was—it was all either an uphill or downward grade—so color me surprised when Henri promptly hailed a taxi to go six blocks.

I climbed in with him, let him give the driver instructions on where to go, then gave my lover a very pointed look.

"This moment makes me ask, why haven't you done that exercise regime Gibs gave you?"

"Because it is inhumane."

As they say, ask a stupid question, get a stupid answer. "Uh-huh. So what's your plan to get around this?"

"The potion is shaping up quite nicely," he returned, meeting me look for look.

It took a second and then I had to bite the inside of my mouth to keep from snickering. "You're developing a fitness potion? Really? How viable is that?"

"More viable than me voluntarily running every day."

I groaned out a laugh. Yeah, okay, he had me there. "How about we find time to go dancing more often together."

"I'll always be delighted to dance with you, dearest."

I made a mental note to drag him out at least once a week—only prayer I had of getting the man into semi-decent shape.

The taxi slowed at the corner and we got out, Henri paying the man. It was only then that I thought to question it.

"Wait, you have this nation's currency?"

"Exchanged it at the hotel's front desk before we left," Henri explained, eyes on the building across the street. "At least some of it."

Such a smart little cookie. I honestly hadn't thought about it until he paid the taxi driver, so it's just as well that he did.

I turned my attention to the building. Oh yeah, this had magical school written all over it. I didn't need magical specs on to see the wards around the place; the air practically vibrated with them. The palace in Kingston had this kind of smell and vibe to it. The building took up a whole city block from what I could see, tan stone that went up three stories. It had a very heavy, gothic feel to it. This was a place of rigid order and tradition. I'd stake my reputation on it.

Henri and I dodged a few cars and carriages as we hopped across the road and up the short staircase to the main door. It wasn't barred so we entered easily, only to fetch up against a very long reception desk manned by three people.

Henri stopped at the first person, a wereowl, with a professional smile. "Royal Mage Davenforth, from Kingston. Is it possible for me to speak to an academic advisor about one of your former students?"

Her head canted at an angle only an owl could pull off without dislocating something. "Is there a problem?"

I flipped my badge open to show it to her, smiling a little apologetically. "This is a murder investigation. One of your graduates died in a different country. We're just trying to get a feel for his background, is all."

"Oh!" she hooted, the surprise evident as her feathers ruffled. "Oh! Oh my. Yes, I can put you in touch with his academic advisor. He'd know best. Who's the person?"

"Mattius Celto," Henri supplied.

"One moment."

In a blink, she whisked away to a room behind her, rattled through a few things, then whisked back to us, a file in her hands. She promptly passed it over to me. "This is Mattius Celto's academic file. I hope it is useful. His advisor would be Ariti. I'll show you to him."

"Thank you so much."

Our guide took us straight down a short hallway right next to the reception area, past several doors, then ended at nearly the last office. She knocked before sticking her head through the open doorway.

"Ariti? Some police are here to ask you questions about a former student."

"Great magic, what's this about?"

She popped out again to usher us in. I tried to allay the man's alarm by giving a smile, but I wasn't sure if it worked. Then again, he seemed to be some form of werelizard? First reptilian were I'd seen. His eyes were on either side of his head and looked wide to me, but that could have been his natural state. His green tail, though, kept twitching on the floor, and that was definitely a sign of agitation.

If someone could write me a guide on all were behavioral tics and what they meant, I'd memorize all one hundred volumes assiduously. Please and thank you.

Henri stepped forward with the introductions once more. "Royal Mage Davenforth from Kingston, sir, at your service. This is my partner from the Queen's Own, Jamie Edwards. We've just a few questions for you regarding Mattius Celto."

At the name, Ariti's expression went from confused to almost...understanding? "Ah. Yes, do be seated. Thank you, Esmelda."

Now that was an interesting reaction.

Our wereowl guide gave a chirp and left.

I settled into a chair, getting my bearings. The room looked oddly enough like my school advisor's office. Full of pictures, books, and knickknacks all shoved onto shelves on the walls. The office was narrow enough that his desk and two chairs for visitors took up all the available space. I'd have serious claustrophobia if I had to work in an office this small.

Henri sat with the file in his lap and a genial expression on his face. "What can you tell me of Celto?"

"The man had larger ambitions than he had the skills or talent for. Frankly, I'm not surprised to hear he got himself into trouble. Students like him often do. They think we're being too harsh on them when we say this isn't the path for you, it's better to find a different vocation. Inevitably, we're proven right in a few years." Ariti shook his head sadly. "Celto especially. He barely scraped the grades together to graduate with the certification that he did. We had to find extra projects and beg some of his professors to round *up* when grading his papers and tests just so he'd pass. He was not a good magical student. If he'd settled for being a hedge wizard, I feel like he'd have progressed far better in that field."

This made sense compared to what I knew of the man. Certainly it fit with what people said of him.

"May I ask what he's being charged with?" Ariti asked with an anticipatory wince.

"It's not that he's being charged with anything," I corrected. "The man was murdered this week."

Ariti's jaw dropped open so much his tongue just about

fell out. "Murdered?!"

"We're trying to figure out why, and who might have had motive. Did he have any enemies here in his home country?"

"I...didn't know him well enough to name names. I can give you a few names of his known associates here, however. I always saw him in the company of two other students."

"That'll help," I said.

He riffled through a few papers on his desk, then in a file in his desk cabinet, before grunting in satisfaction. "I couldn't remember their first names. José Diakos and Rile Hasapi. You should know that Diakos dropped out shortly before Celto graduated. His grades were even worse than Celto's. I believe he went into a family business of some sort? Hasapi was the only decent magician of the three of them, but he's middling at best. He went into pharmacy as a tech."

Ah, one of those. I knew a little about this because of the factory workers explaining to me what a tech did. Basically, they were over herb prep, everything from growing to harvesting to basic canning or ingredient preparation. It was grunt work but apparently well-paid grunt work. Anyone without the magical talent to make it doing actual spell work resorted to jobs like this.

I jotted all of this down, double-checking against the file that I had spelled the name right because of course it was in a native language and not an alphabet I really knew. There were days I cursed Belladonna for everything she did to my body, and then other days where I lamented the lack of upgrades. Really? She gave me a blanket translation spell on my ears but couldn't just do my eyes as well?

I digressed.

Henri had his own questions. "I understand that he was not knowledgeable about herbs in Dolivo. What about herbology here?"

"As I said, middling at best. Celto was a decent brewer at primary levels, which is why I tried to get him to be a hedge wizard. To no avail, in the end. He was one of those students who could be textbook perfect if you gave him all the materials and simple instructions to follow. He just didn't grasp the mechanics behind it all, or so his professors complained to me."

Ah, one of THOSE. I got it now.

Ariti's eyes darted between us. "You keep asking about potions, so was that how Celto got himself into trouble?"

"There's a strong possibility of that, we shall say." I phrased what came out of my mouth next semi-carefully. "What's really puzzling us is how we found him. He was the supervisor in a medical potions factory. He supposedly invented a cure for consumption and was manufacturing it there."

For the second time, Ariti's jaw dropped, and then he spluttered out half-formed denials before he managed to land on one. "No. No, absolutely not. He didn't have the skills for that. It wasn't just the knowledge he was lacking, it was the talent and understanding of potions. There's no way under the sun he came up with something like that!"

Henri gave a grunt. "Yes, I tend to agree just from what I saw of him up there. On the résumé he handed his supporters in Dolivo, it showed that he worked as a Potions lab assistant here at the school while a student. May we speak to his supervisor?"

Another blank look. "What? No, he never worked in a Potions lab here. To start with, he didn't have the grades for it."

"Ah-haaaa," I intoned. "Another lie. I take it your lab people have to be top tier?"

"Certainly something above an almost-failing average."

Henri winced in understanding. "Indeed. Where did he work, anywhere?"

Ariti had to think about it. "I don't remember him holding any job through the school. As I said, he didn't have the grades for it. He might have held a job while studying here, but I can't swear to that. This was a few years ago."

And he'd slept since then, got it.

I was out of questions for him, so I gave Ariti a smile and

shifted to stand. "Thank you so much, sir, you've shed a lot of light on Celto for me."

"I'm happy to help, it's just...not news I was expecting. Oh! Has his family been notified?"

"We'll stop by the police station and make sure that happens," I promised. "Er...where is the nearest police station?"

"Just down this street"—he pointed right—"and down two blocks."

"Thank you so much."

Henri handed back the student file and we left at that point, me tucking my arm through his just because I wanted to. We waved goodbye to the receptionist, as she'd been nice, and it wasn't until we were out of the building and back on the sidewalk that either of us looked at each other.

"So," I said.

"So," he agreed. "Celto was definitely not the inventor. Now, where did he lay hands on this, I wonder?"

"That is a question I'd very much like an answer to."

Report 14: A Difficult Interview

The police station was very easy to find indeed and on the larger size, which made sense considering the population of the city. We were in a proper city this time, something on par with Kingston. The thrum and noise of it alone left that impression on me. The police station was a reflection of this, as the main building stood three stories tall, was made of sandstone, and had two outlier buildings further back from the street. Or at least, two more that I could see through the black iron fence.

I held the door open for Jamie before stepping through myself. The reception area was short and barely held more than a welcoming desk to the right and a line of chairs bracketing the wall to the left.

A bored looking junior officer greeted Jamie. "Can I help you?"

That was indeed the question.

Jamie fielded it with her usual polite smile and show of her badge. "Jamie Edwards, Queen's Own from Kingston. Can I speak with one of your detectives?"

The officer took one look at the badge and straightened, now looking confused. "Yes, er, Agent? What's this about?"

"We're here investigating a murder. We'd rather keep it all in jurisdiction, so I'm here to report what we're doing and borrow one of your detectives if at all possible."

"Uhh..."

I could see two brain cells collide, ricochet off each other, and end in a failed connection. The poor boy had no idea what to make of this request or to whom to field it.

Fortunately for him, a detective nearby took note of this and turned, her head canted in question. She looked like a shadow in a way, the black uniform on her body blending in almost perfectly with her dark skin. It was unusual to see a Svartálfar in this area of the world, but like Gerring, she was no doubt very welcome in the officers' ranks. Dark Elves made excellent policemen.

She approached with a sharp evaluation of me and Jamie—not hostile, just very curious. "I'm sorry, you're from where?"

"Kingston, Wolstenholme," Jamie repeated. "Unusual, I know, for someone to be up here for this, but this whole case is unusual. I'm Jamie Edwards. This is my partner, Henri Davenforth."

"Nova Woods, Homicide. Why don't you follow me to my desk and if I can't help you, I can at least introduce you to someone who can."

Amenable to this, I followed the two women to a corner of the very busy bullpen. A drunk and disorderly consisting of half a ship's crew was disturbing most of the room, with sailors being dragged off one by one to a holding cell. I ignored it with the ease of long practice.

There were three simple wooden chairs sitting next to a battered desk in danger of collapse under the weight of all the files stacked upon it. It had a sense of organized chaos, like most detectives' desks.

I took one chair, Jamie the other, and Detective Woods settled into her accustomed chair.

"From the top, if you would," Woods requested.

I handled the explanation as succinctly as I knew how, then ended, not sure if she was able to help us or not.

Woods blinked at me, then Jamie, before turning back to me. "So, one of my countrymen got himself murdered—you think because he stole the patent of a very expensive potion—in Dolivo. You've tracked him backwards to here because you want to interview friends and family, see where he could have possibly laid hands on this."

"Or if he had any enemies that would follow him to Dolivo," Jamie tacked on. "Really, we're not sure where he got the potion from. We just know he didn't have the skills to create it. For all I know, some other family member made it and gave him the recipe."

"What's this man's name again? Mattius Celto?"

"Correct."

She stood again. "I don't think we've gotten notice he's dead, let me double-check that. We'll need to notify family first and foremost. As for who can help you—I don't think anyone specifically is in charge of foreign affairs like this. I'll take you on. I'm very curious how this will play out."

"We appreciate that, thanks." Jamie watched her go for a moment before leaning in closer to my side and murmuring, "Now who dropped the ball in notifying next of kin? That should have been done well before we got here."

"That is a very good question. We'll follow up on that, assuming she's correct."

Woods came back in fifteen minutes, all while shaking her head. "I'm sadly correct. I figured anyone who died on foreign soil under circumstances like this would have made break room gossip if nothing else. We do not have record he died. If you don't mind, let me grab the forms to notify next of kin. After those are done, I'll take you with me and we can try to catch the family."

"Of course," I assured her.

The forms were simple and not far different than

the ones we used in Kingston. Jamie couldn't read a word, of course the language was different here, but I could, so I took over the pen. It took mere moments to fill them out before handing them over again. Nova filed them, looked up the next of kin in a very large address book, and then took us out a side door and into a parking lot of vehicles.

Mentally praying she was not perfectly insane like my lover, I climbed into the backseat. Jamie took the passenger side in the front and settled in comfortably as Detective Woods drove us at a sedate pace to the main street. I held my breath until she joined traffic, but she never tried to hurry matters along, seemingly content to match the speed of the other drivers.

Oh good, a sensible driver. I let out a prayer of silent thanks and dared to relax.

Woods inquired of Jamie over the road noise, "Clarify this for me. You said your queen is a shareholder in this business of Celto's and that's why you were sent up?"

"Well, Queen Regina and the second prince of Dolivo. They wanted a proper investigation done, and the police in the town haven't had a murder in living memory. They were quick to concede they needed help."

"Ah-ha. Who else do you want to talk to aside from family, or do you know yet?"

"Two school friends. I have their names."

"Good, good. I'm glad you stopped by and talked to me first."

"Well, jurisdiction, after all."

"There's that as well."

Woods was the amiable sort, apparently. It did make our lives easier. She could have thrown a fit about us trying to investigate in her own territory, but she saw sense in finding the murderer instead.

"You're running out of time today," Woods told us.

"And I don't have an address for the two friends besides, but we can at least talk to your victim's family."

Running out of time...? Oh yes, of course, until the end of her shift. It was nearing the dinner hour.

Woods drove us confidently to the back area of the foothills and into a somewhat modest area of town. Not poor—definitely not on the "wrong side," as people phrased it—just not affluent. The streetlamps were spaced very far apart, the roads clean for the most part but with stacks of rubbish near the bins, and most of the houses could use a fresh coat of paint. Still, I'd been in worse areas of a city. Routinely, at that.

We pulled in tight against a curb in front of a two-story townhouse of sandstone. Forensics would be required to tell what kind of plant was dying in the window boxes. I heard lively chatter and a call to stop that nonsense from inside. Indeed, if this was Celto's family house, I didn't see any signs of mourning here.

Woods popped out, double-checked an address she had written in her notebook, and gave a grunt of satisfaction. "This is the place. I better notify them."

As she was in the right uniform to do so, I waved her on.

Woods gave the wooden door a sharp rap with her knuckles.

There had been little left of Celto's features after taking a bomb directly to the front, so I couldn't speak much of resemblance, but the woman who answered had the right age to be his mother. She had a matronly shape to her, brown hair in a bun that was escaping in tendrils, a stained apron tied around her waist. She took in a policewoman and two foreigners with a blink and then looked nervous.

"Hello, can I help you?"

"Are you Mrs. Celto, Mattius Celto's mother?" Woods asked gently.

"I am, yes. Why, is Mattius in trouble?"

For her, that would have been far preferable to what Woods would say next. My heart ached in sympathy for her.

"Mrs. Celto, I'm so sorry to tell you this. Mattius Celto died several days ago in Dolivo."

She stared at Woods as if her words were nonsensical. Nothing in them connected. When they did, it was with horror and a muted wail of denial, her knees giving out from under her.

Jamie was a speeding blur at my side, there and gone again in a displacement of air. She caught the mother before she could hit the ground, an arm solidly around her waist, her own chest propping the woman up.

From inside the house, I could hear the sound of a man half-running.

"Hazel? Hazel, what's wrong?"

Ah, the husband. I hoped he wasn't also a fainter.

The man's build was massive, much like a beer keg on legs, his bushy mustache obscuring half of his face. His eyes, though, took us in with one sweep and tightened. He knew in that moment that whatever brought us here wasn't good. He dipped down, caught up his wife in strong arms, and hauled her further into the house.

"Come in, officers. Come in and tell me what you said to my wife."

That last sounded a bit like a threat. I wasn't too concerned. I didn't think he'd be violent after he heard what we had to say.

Mrs. Celto clung to her husband, silent tears leaking out. She tried several times to speak, her throat too constricted to get anything out at first. She didn't manage it until her husband had her on the couch.

I followed them in and saw two children under the age of ten and a worried looking girl who might be an older cousin. Or Mattius Celto's younger sister.

I warned the mother, "It would be best to take the children into another room. They shouldn't hear this."

The mother grimaced in agreement and shoed the eldest of the three on. She gave an uncertain nod before taking both children in hand and ushering them into a back room somewhere out of sight.

The living room was cramped with two couches and a single chair. I took the other couch with Jamie, leaving Woods the chair, and we settled as Mrs. Celto finally found her voice.

"They said Matt's dead," she managed in a threadbare voice, her hands still clutching her husband close.

His jaw dropped and he turned sharply to me. "What? That's not possible. We spoke to him just over a week ago!"

"I'm so sorry," I returned as gently as I knew how. "I believe you spoke to him right before he was killed. I can verify that it was indeed your son, as I was the one who did his autopsy."

Woods looked at me with keen interest. Hadn't expected that of me, for some reason. Granted, physical forensics weren't usually my forte, but I'd done a magical examination on his body, not a physical one.

The father's face crumbled and grief set in. "Why? What happened?"

Jamie stirred at my side. "We're still trying to figure out why. I can tell you what happened, but please, answer some questions for us? We need more facts to figure this out."

Mrs. Celto rallied and gave Jamie a firm nod. She stared at her as if somehow Jamie held answers that might make this horrible situation better. "What happened?"

Jamie and I shared a look. It was never pleasant telling someone what had happened, but in this case… the method of murder was so brutal. It wouldn't go over well.

"I want you to understand first that your son's death was immediate and painless. Alright? The method was...not good, but he was dead instantly." Jamie took in a breath and then calmly laid it out. "We found him in his office in the factory. He'd taken a magical mini-bomb to the chest."

Mrs. Celto reached for straws. "An experiment gone wrong...?"

"No, ma'am, I'm sorry. This was deliberate murder. Someone was incredibly wroth with your son. What we're struggling to figure out is *why*. It wasn't just Mattius attacked, you see, but another shareholder he was having a meeting with."

Mr. Celto found his voice, rough and deep with pain. "Not just my son? So this person killed two people?"

"Not quite, although he tried. The other victim managed to survive." I wasn't sure how they'd take that news.

Mrs. Celto wiped away tears. "Thank all the gods for that. I wouldn't want another parent grieving a child lost. But how did the other person survive?"

"She put on a protection charm before coming into the factory. It mitigated most of the damage done by the bomb. I'm sorry to say your son wasn't wearing one. Without it, he had no such protections." I leaned forward a touch, looking at both of them with sympathy. "I can only imagine the pain you're going through. I promise you, we're doing all we can to find out who did this. We just don't know enough right now to figure out the motive. Can I ask you a few questions?"

I used 'can' instead of 'may' because I honestly didn't know if they were up to such questioning at this time.

Mr. Celto met my eyes levelly. "Please do, Detective."

"First, the origin of the potion Mattius was making up north is in question. Where did it come from?"

"Oh, it was..." Mrs. Celto glanced at her husband as she answered. "It was a school project, that's what Mattius said."

Jamie and I exchanged another look. Obviously didn't come from the family. He'd lied to his parents about where the potion had come from.

Mr. Celto caught our exchange and challenged it. "Is that not right?"

"I'm sorry, sir, it's not." I mentally prayed he didn't throw me out of the house for what I needed to say next. "I'm not here to cast aspersions against the dead, you understand. It's just that we're fairly sure the potion is the lynchpin to this case. The patent for it was stolen from your son's office, which suggests to me that it was the primary motive for his murder. Also, in investigating your son's background, I found nothing to indicate he would have either the knowledge or skills to make such a potion."

The parents knew their son, at least. They didn't look too surprised at my confusion.

Mrs. Celto bit her lip before offering, "It wasn't that one of his friends helped him?"

"If they did, they weren't mentioned. Mattius presented himself as the sole creator."

Another weighty moment of silence. This one looked more like regret.

Rubbing a hand over his face, Mr. Celto said, "He was always trying to cut corners, even as a child. We'd hoped, when he got the backing for this project, that he'd finally straightened out his life. We didn't have to worry about him anymore."

Ah. Now this made more sense. They were trying not to look a gift horse in the mouth.

Jamie phrased her words with diplomacy. "Potions didn't seem to be your son's strong suit. We didn't find any indication that he did his own potions, even at home. Can I ask if his friends were better at it?

Or someone he might be acquainted with who knew potions and herbs?"

The parents winced again.

The mother answered, "Not really. They all struggled through those courses in school. Mattius really did do a potion project under a professor, though. It was one of those things he worked on to improve his grade."

Now, that sounded like a more plausible lead. If he stole the potion from a professor it would make more sense. "Do you remember which professor?"

She spread her hands helplessly. "I'm sorry, he did so many projects like that. I rarely heard which professor. His friends will know, though. They worked on it with him."

Jamie flipped a page in her notebook. "José Diakos and Rile Hasapi, correct? Any other friends?"

"Well, yes, but those are the two that he went to school with." Mr. Celto ran a hand over his face and looked both heartsick and exhausted, his face drawn and pale. "I'd hate to think it was my son's greed that killed him, but that's what it looks like, doesn't it? Because he took something that wasn't his, he was killed for it."

I didn't want to say as much aloud, but I feared that was exactly the case. "When I can find the origin of that potion, I'll be able to answer that question for you. For now, it's just strange that the patent is gone. It could well be that it went missing before his death and no one knew about it. It's not something you'd track day to day, after all."

He nodded but didn't look convinced. To be perfectly frank, neither was I.

The mother knew where both school friends lived, and Woods jotted down directions for us so we could interview them later. I offered condolences once more, and directions to our hotel so they could call on us if they thought of anything else. People often did after such interviews, when their heads had had a chance to clear.

Mrs. Celto caught Jamie's hand before we left, stalling her just inside the door.

"Detective, my son may have done something he shouldn't have, but he didn't deserve to die for it. Please find who did this."

Jamie gripped her hand in return and smiled. "I promise you, we won't let this case go until we get an answer. Murder is never justified. We'll find who did this."

A tear tracked down the mother's cheek as she mustered a smile in return. She let go and retreated into her house to mourn with her family.

We returned to the car and it was then that the three of us took a moment.

"It says something that neither parent was surprised to hear their son might have stolen that potion." I shook my head sadly. "Just how much trouble did he cause as a child?"

"A lot, apparently." Jamie grimaced. "I bet he was something like Eddy. Full of mischief and without any kind of outlet for it."

Dear great magic, that was a terrifying thought. Eddy Jameson was already a handful and he didn't have a magical spark in his entire body. I shuddered to think of such an individual.

Woods' gaze bounced between us. "You're really sure he stole the potion, aren't you? And that he was killed to get it back."

Jamie's expression and tone turned wry. "The guy barely passed school but suddenly knew how to use foreign herbs to create a complex potion that cures consumption a year later. A potion he couldn't even recreate on his own, mind you. What's that look like to you, Officer?"

Woods pursed her lips in a silent whistle. "Oh, he

definitely stole it, then. No question. Who'd he steal it from?"

"Now, that is the million-crown question."

Report 15: Street Food!

As usual, my foodie pulls through.

One must have priorities in life.

Absolutely. Food is one of them.

So glad to see the couple in agreement.

Henri assured us that the best food in this city, bar none, was to be found in the open-air market along the wharf. Since he was the only one who had been here before, we chose to believe him and followed him right down to the coastline. It was a short walk from the hotel—three blocks maybe—and all downhill, so we walked. The cats trotted at our heels, as they wanted to get out and explore too after all the sunbathing that morning.

Since we were in casual mode, we chose to act like tourists for a night. I exchanged money before leaving the hotel and had every intention of buying some souvenirs. Might as well, right? Some of those souvenirs would be spices. For me. I am my target audience.

The secret was out about this place, clearly, as the wharf was jam-packed with people. The opening onto the street had a nice arch, a wooden structure lit up with a sign announcing the location in a foreign script I couldn't begin to read. People were flowing inside and, from the glimpse I could get over people's heads, the crowd moved at a shuffle once they entered.

Henri turned his head to address everyone following. "If you get separated from the rest of us, come back here and wait. We'll find you. Absolutely do not eat every sample handed to you unless you have a very high spice tolerance. If you hold up a pinky and get a nod in return, then it's very spicy. My mother, whose spice tolerance is legendary in the family, nearly fainted the first time she put a regularly spiced dish in her mouth in this country."

Oh wow. Uh, I was good with spice, but not to that level. I considered myself forewarned.

How a pinky came to mean super spicy, death incoming, that was my question.

Cultures, man.

I held hands with Henri as we dove into the crowd, sticking close because I kinda liked him.

Henri pointed to the side. "The one-pan rice is always a good choice here. It's flavorful and they never season it to be hot. If they have multiple pans going, as this vendor does, then it's a good indication there's multiple choices in meat. Most likely seafood or chicken."

"I'm famished, so let's hit him first."

The vendors were stacked side by side, forming a solid row. There seemed to be just enough space between for them to stack up supplies or put in ovens and such, but it was tight quarters for them. I had a hard time differentiating the smell of the fried rice from everything else around me. The place was packed with scents. Every meat you could think of was grilling here, breads of all sorts, the rice of course, some sort of sweets further down…? I think. My poor nose was overwhelmed trying to sort it all. It was a good sort of problem to have.

We all got fried rice—I got the crab version—which came in a paper funnel concoction with a wooden stick that acted as a spoon. Happy, I stuffed my face as we continued our walk.

It wasn't just food here, although about half the vendors offered some sort of gastric pleasure. There were pretty stained glass displays, jewelry of all sorts, some really fun-looking blankets in that large cable knit. I liked too many things that would be bulky and hard to carry.

To Henri, I inquired hopefully, "Will we need to come out the same way we came in?"

He regarded me quizzically. "No, the wharf has another exit in this direction. Most people catch a taxi back after walking through. Why?"

"Oh. Rats. Uh, well, there's pretty things we're passing that I'd like to buy. But most of them are too large. It would be hard to carry them all in this crowd."

"Ahh, I see. In fact, most vendors offer delivery for a small fee. Assuming you're within a certain radius of the wharf, which we are."

This sparked joy.

He could see the delight on my face. His smile was full of affection. "What caught your eye, my dear?"

"That pretty stained glass back there and the thick green blanket at the vendor next to it."

Niamh leaned in over my shoulder, her tone full of interest, "Can we really get things delivered to the hotel?"

"We did upon my last visit here, which was some six, seven years ago?"

Niamh and I exchanged a look and a firm nod. Pretties. Must have.

We promptly turned and doubled back to the vendors in question. The stained glass vendor looked like a kind of weredragon? Of some sort? This world didn't have dragons, but the vendor sure looked it to my eye. They ducked their (her?) head in a smile and greeted us warmly.

"Welcome, welcome. We have many things here to see. If there is something you like on display but you wish it in a different size or color, please tell me. I have a shop of inventory that I can pull from."

Well, now, that was good to know. I stepped onto the rug that signified her interior shop space, small as it was. "Do you deliver?"

"Within a certain area."

Henri poked his head around me to tell her, "We're at the Overlook Hotel."

"Yes, that's within range."

Oh, goodie.

I went straight for the glass pane that depicted a fairy rising from a flower in a wooded setting. The colors were stunning and I really wanted this hanging in my bedroom window. I glanced at the price and, while it was high, I wasn't too surprised. Good artwork costs something.

Some part of my mind dinged, the responsible adult in me remembering a goal I had for this evening. Namely, to expose Eddy properly to this culture and get him used to converting currency in his head. It would be a vital skill for him later. I turned, found him eyeing a glass paperweight in lava colors with interest.

"Eddy."

He looked up, then back down again. "Jamie, can I buy this? It's so wicked."

"You can buy whatever you have the money for, but come here first. Actually, bring that with you."

He promptly scooped it up and brought it carefully with him, cradling it with both hands. It was a sizeable paperweight, heavy enough by the look of it to make a good murder weapon.

Look, the hazard of my profession was that I judged everything by its lethality, okay?

I asked the shopkeeper, "Do you mind if we do a quick currency lesson? I want him to learn how to do this."

She nodded, pleased, her fingers clacking together. The scales at the ends made a sharp clicking noise. "Wise of you. Wise. Not all parents teach a child like this. Young man, you like my paperweight. What is the price on it?"

"Uhh...it says twenty-three?"

"What is the currency of this country?"

Eddy looked at her blankly. "I have no idea."

"Let's start there," our vendor suggested.

I listened as she succinctly laid out the coinage, the currency rates for the day, and then prompted Eddy to do the math. When he struggled to do it in his head, she produced a pad and pencil and let him scratch it out. He did better with the visual.

It was very sweet of her, and I promised myself to tip her well for being such a good sport.

Eddy got his paperweight, I got my stained glass fairy,

and Niamh picked up a very cool lamp shade that was all sorts of pretty, like a Tiffany lamp. Evans was at the vendor next door, hands full of fluffy, soft things.

With the delivery set up, wares paid for, I ducked next door to join Evans. Or that was the plan, anyway. I got a whole three steps outside when I saw a drunk hassling a smaller pixie. He was belligerent and I could smell the alcohol on him even at this distance.

Here's the thing. The translation spell on me let me understand every word said but it didn't downplay accents. I could more or less tell people's regions from the way they pronounced things. It came in handy sometimes, like now.

The drunk had a distinctly Kingstonian accent.

"—I *dropped* it, I said! Gimme another one."

"Sir, you dropping it has nothing to do with me. If you want another, then purchase another."

"Don't give me that lip! I said I dropped it, I didn't get a single bite, so gimme another!"

Okay, look, I know I'm not technically from Kingston. Still, I'd made it my home, so to me, this was a shameful display from one of my countrymen. It embarrassed me just to listen to this nonsense. The guy was likely a sailor on shore leave, and they were known to cause trouble, but still.

I couldn't ignore it and let it slide. The pixie was half the guy's size, and drunks didn't know their own strength. No one else was willing to help; they were giving the two a wide berth, trying to avoid getting entangled in the situation.

Shaking my head, I marched in and pulled out my cop voice. "Sir. Sir!"

Drunkard looked at me blearily, taking me in with a sneer. Ever look at someone and wonder who tied their shoelaces for them? Yeah. That was my visual.

"You stay out of this, whore."

"Oh, you did not." Seriously, I hated drunkards. Hated them.

He got right in my face—which, ewww, breath was foul—and tried to loom over me. "You stay *out of this*."

This Potion is Da Bomb 143

"You're too drunk to even realize how much of a jerk you're being right now. Go back to your hotel."

He didn't like that I was holding my ground. Of course, he didn't realize I could crack him like a glowstick over my knee, either. Most men didn't until they saw me in action.

I could hear the shopkeeper ask Henri behind me, "Aren't you going to help her?"

"If it looks like he's in need of being rescued from her," Henri returned calmly, "then I'll step in."

I did love that man. His response made me smile.

Of course, Drunkard didn't like this either. He got even more belligerent and tried to loom more.

"I *said*—"

I pulled out my badge and waved it in front of his face. It took a second—it was so close that his eyes went cross-eyed as he tried to focus—and then all color just drained south. I'd seen corpses with better color.

"You were saying?" I prompted politely. Well, I tried. Controlling my tongue was no issue, but my face sure needed deliverance.

The man backed down fast, putting distance between us and looking all sorts of hangdog. "No, Kingsman. I'm sorry."

I considered correcting him for all of a nanosecond and decided to let it ride. "First, apologize to the vendor, because you were seriously out of line."

He promptly turned and gave the man a muttered apology.

Just like a toddler, this one. Ugh, I hated drunks. "Now. I'd like to help you out. Which way did you come in?"

"I can take myself to my hotel, Kingsman."

"Good. Go directly there. Do not pass Go, do not collect two hundred dollars. You go back to your room, sober up, and *stay sober*. If there's report of a Kingston sailor causing trouble, I will know it's you and will come after your hide. Clear?"

"Yes, ma'am." He gave me an awkward bow, turned on a heel, and toddled off.

The vendor put a hand over his heart and gave a sigh of relief. "Thank you, ma'am, so much. I was afraid he'd get violent."

"I was too, which was why I stepped in. Which shop is yours?"

He indicated one that sold a variety of snacks, most of them of the nut variety. What caught my attention was the row of glass bottles that looked like spices. Oooh, now, there was something I could get into. I pointed to it and asked hopefully, "Are those spices for sale?"

"Yes. Oh, are you interested? Please, please, I'll give you a discount for your help."

"Just deliver them for free and we'll call it even. Henri!" I turned, hailing him. "Henri, he has fun-looking spices!"

Henri approached, weaving his way between people as he came, and we stood at the front of the shop with saliva pooling in our mouths. Well, at least, mine certainly was. Yum, yum, yum.

The vendor was so grateful he bent over backward to be helpful. As a result, I ended up with two bags full of spices and a cup of free roasted nuts. The nuts were especially delightful, and he told me which seasoning he used on them, so I bought three bottles. Henri only indulged me because, foodie that he was, he not only approved of my spending half my wallet here, but knew that he would benefit down the line.

I turned and left with a satisfied smile. Now. What other fun things could I get into? Ooh, that looked sparkly down there. Wait, I had to get the blanket before I got sidetracked again.

Evans darted to my side from nowhere, looking more than panicked.

"Jamie, I can't find Eddy. And my wallet is gone."

Uh-oh. I forgot to give Eddy limits on pickpocketing Evans.

My bad.

I looked down and around, realized I saw Clint, and Henri had Phil on his shoulder, but we were short a cat. "And we're missing Tasha. Niamh! You got Tasha?"

Niamh was a little further down from us at a store. At my hail, she looked up and then around before shaking her head. "No, why?"

"We're missing a wallet, Eddy, and Tasha." In a foreign open market. Oh boy. In retrospect, I should have put a leash on Eddy.

Henri patted my shoulder. "Not to worry, my dear. I put a tracking spell on Jameson. Hopefully he has Tasha."

First I'd heard of this. "Wait, you did? When?"

"Oh, right, you did," Evans chimed in with clear relief. "I'd forgotten that. You've kept it on him since Dolivo?"

"I feared losing him in a foreign country. I thought it best to take precautions."

Yeah, we were working on Eddy's impulsiveness. Just as well Henri took precautions. I was sure Niamh could track him down eventually but Henri's tracking spell would be faster than forcing her to wade through all these auras in a crowded place.

Niamh doubled back to us. "Do I need to track him?"

"I've a tracking spell on Jameson," Henri repeated. "But track Tasha, in case they aren't together."

"Alright."

"Tasha's back here!" Clint called to me.

I turned, jogging back to the area I'd heard his voice from, and found that I wasn't the only one who really liked those soft looking blankets. Tasha had crawled right up into the display and somehow curled one around her, looking like sushi cat.

She blinked up at me with liquid gold eyes, the hope in them clear. "Can has?"

Whelp. Can't argue with that. "Sure, I guess. Since you already got fur all over it."

She purred in contentment.

Well, that was one down. I just had to find the other one missing.

If luck was with us, Eddy wouldn't have spent Evans' entire wallet by the time we caught up with him.

You did NOT put Jameson onto pickpocketing Evans.

It was supposed to be just practice!
I guess I didn't explain it well enough.

You're not going to have him do that to me, are you?

No, you're too easy a mark.

I beg your pardon!

Even I heard about your one-year-old nephew stealing from you, Davenforth.

see?

Oh, for mercy's sake.

Report 16: ~~Interview with Friends~~
He's Dead, Jim

??? That is not what I named the chapter.
Star Trek next for you. You must get this reference.

We set out with Woods early the next morning to do interviews. She was kind enough to pick us up, negating the need for a taxi. Jamie and I left everyone else at the hotel, as we could hardly split duties with Woods needing to escort us. I needed someone to supervise Jameson while he studied and, yes, he'd gotten a scolding from Evans and now swore to be on his best behavior. But the kid could write the book about good intentions.

I'd personally believe it when I saw it, but that was neither here nor there. He was Evans' problem until our return.

Our attempt to interview José Diakos was quickly thwarted. He was at neither house nor workplace, apparently on a vacation with his wife and not expected back for some days. We'd come back to him if time allowed. Workplace verified he worked the days Celto was killed, so I knew he wasn't a suspect. I'd still like to talk to him if possible, though.

The other friend of Celto, Rile Hasapi, we found at his workplace. It was a commercial greenhouse that grew common herbs used for pharmaceutical purposes. For Hasapi's education and talent, a job like this was perfect.

We stopped in at the front office, which was nothing more than a lean-to on the side of the greenhouse with a desk and two chairs inside, a file cabinet shoved into the corner. The woman at the desk had protective cuffs over her sleeves that went up to her elbows, a streak of dirt along one furry cheek. She blinked up at us with golden eyes, then focused on Woods.

"If some thrice-cursed fool working for me got a drunk and disorderly again, I'm not bailing them out," she announced flatly.

Oh dear. There was an auspicious beginning.

Woods negated this with a smile. "Not here for that sort of trouble. I'm Detective Woods. This is Edwards and Davenforth, special agents from Kingston. We just need to talk to Hasapi."

"Hasapi?" she repeated blankly. "You're naming the one employee I *don't* have trouble with."

"He's not in trouble now," Jamie assured her. "He knows my victim and I want to ask some questions."

"Ohhh. Good. Hate to lose one of my more reliable employees. Come on through, I'll take you to him. He's working the back section today, rebuilding some shelves." She stood and moved stiffly to the side, her gait awkward.

It took me a few seconds to realize that she was suffering from either an injury or arthritis in her lower joints, hence the stiffness. I didn't mean to stare, but she must have caught my expression as she gave me a wry smile.

"Irony, eh? Here I grow and sell medical herbs but can't get a decent potion for arthritis. Mine wears out in four hours or so. Don't mind me. I'm Guzzman, by the way, nice to meet you."

We followed her out the door and into the cooler, damper interior of the greenhouse. I saw several rain-collecting barrels tucked in along the roof, all of them powered by charms to keep a fine mist over certain herbs. It was well laid out, methodical with all the beds raised on tables. The scent of earth and plant life was strong in my nostrils—not unpleasant.

When Guzzman said Hasapi was in the back, she'd

not meant it figuratively. He was behind the building and beside a smaller one, standing at a work table, something that looked much like a work shed. He had tools laid out and was cutting wood with a steady hand. I took him in from head to toe. His skin was darker than his countrymen, likely from being outdoors so much, black hair plastered to his scalp from sweat, much like the white shirt he wore. Not a handsome man, not plain, the sort of average looking man that was hard to describe.

He paused at our entrance and gave his boss a look askance. "Guzzman, we got a special order?"

"No, they're here for you. You're not in trouble, but they have some questions."

From the look on Hasapi's face, he couldn't fathom why we were here but he did put the tools down so he could face us properly, moving to stand in the sun as he did so.

Jamie pulled her badge and showed it to him. "I really do only have some questions for you. You know my victim, you see. I'm Jamie Edwards, Queen's Own from Kingston. This is my partner, Royal Mage Henri Davenforth. Officer Woods is here to keep things legal for us."

Hasapi did not like this much law enforcement here to speak with him—the way his eyes grew a trifle round was good indication of that—but he gamely gave us a nod. "Uh, nice to meet you. I know your victim, you said?"

As gently as I could, I informed him, "One of your old school friends, Mattius Celto, was killed last week. My condolences."

Hasapi looked away for a long moment, eyes bright, jaw working. "Celto? Dark souls, *why*? He didn't have it in him to harm anyone!"

"The why is very much in question. We came to speak with you because of it." Jamie pulled out her notebook but didn't try to write anything down just yet. "How in touch were you with him?"

"After school? Not very. We met up sometimes for drinks, but Celto was always between temporary jobs. Made it hard to know if he was in town or not. About eight months or so ago, I lost track of him completely. His parents could only tell me he'd gotten a very good job in Dolivo and they hoped to have him home for the holidays. I thought I'd catch up with him…then…" He trailed off sadly, shoulders dropping.

Ah, the truest regrets were always the things we wanted to do and never did. This poor man would never have a drink with his friend again. I felt some sympathy for him.

Hasapi straightened, sniffling. "If you're here talking to me, then he wasn't killed in an accident."

"No," I confirmed. "He was murdered. He was the factory supervisor over a potion in Dolivo."

Hasapi's head shook in little micro movements, confusion and denial warring over his face. "A factory supervisor? For potions?"

"I think you know as well as I do that he didn't have the qualifications for it."

"Uh, no. I mean, the man was my friend, but he and potions? The two were not a good mix. He barely passed Potions in school. I was the best of the group when it came down to herbology—it's why I'm working here." Hasapi rubbed a hand along the back of his neck and looked disturbed now. "How did he get the job?"

"Well, he invented a potion to cure a common illness." Jamie lifted her eyebrow and waited a second.

Hasapi stared back at her. The man could not have been more flummoxed.

"You know he didn't have the skills to do that," I prompted.

"No way in the wide green world," Hasapi agreed faintly. "I'm almost scared to ask more questions. I mean, I'd hate to speak ill of him, but...he didn't have that kind of talent with potions. I wouldn't have spent half our time tutoring him in school if he had."

At least the man was honest. "If I say that the potion he introduced to the world cured consumption, would that ring any bells for you?"

It did, that was obvious in a glance. Hasapi straightened immediately, mouth open in astonishment.

"Yes. Yes, I know that potion. It wasn't something Celto made, though. Well, I guess he helped some because he was a lab assistant for it during one semester, but that was Professor Soto's baby."

Even as Jamie wrote the name down, she pushed him further. "Professor Soto? Can you give me a brief physical description of him? Anything you know, too."

"Sure. He's a little shorter than average height, slender, hair's close cropped and white. His skin's always tanned from being outside so much. He's older, maybe seventies? But he's not stooped, he's still very active and fit, especially for his age. He was our Potions professor for most of the last year. Brilliant man, absolutely brilliant. Taught us just for the fun of it. Said he was retired and bored and didn't have anything better to do. The consumption potion was his pet project, something he had us working on, as he kept varying up ingredients and herbs, trying to find some unique combination. What for, he never said. I think..." Hasapi furrowed his brow as he thought hard. "I think he had a grant for it the last semester because he paid me a stipend for the help. Not Celto, though. Well, and it made sense—Celto was there to help improve his grade. I actually did do some legwork for Professor Soto so I'd earned the paycheck."

I could not be more elated. Finally, a solid lead. If the professor truly did have a grant for this potion, he must have had a patent as well, which meant a paper trail at the patent office. I couldn't wait to go digging through their files next."

Hasapi faltered, looking between us uncertainly. "I'm afraid to ask. Did Celto say it was his? His potion?"

"He was the only one credited." Jamie shrugged and let him come to his own conclusion.

Hasapi just sighed, shoulders slumping again. "Blighted fool. Always tyring to get rich quick, no matter that it always got him into trouble, in the end. I hope it wasn't the reason he was killed. I'm afraid to ask, have you spoken to his parents yet? Do they know all of this?"

"They do."

Wincing, Hasapi muttered, "I'll stop by after work and offer my condolences, at least. See if I can do anything for them. Agents, I don't know what else to tell you. I didn't know what he was up to. I wish I had, I would have talked him out of it. I can say for sure that the potion was Professor Soto's. You said Dolivo was where the factory was? Were they using Dolivian herbs?"

I nodded. "They were."

"Then it was definitely the professor's. That was the last variation we worked on. I remember because it was deucedly hard to find the herbs he wanted in local stores. Had to special order one of them. I did a lot of errand running for him."

It was good to have all of that confirmed. I thrilled at having a lead. Although how a retired potions professor did all the running about and such necessary to kill Celto was currently a mystery. Unless he'd hired someone?

Jamie took out a card and handed it to him. "If you think of anything, contact us at the Overlook Hotel. We'll be there the next two days or so. If you can't find us there, you can contact my office and they'll forward the message to me. Again, I'm sorry for the death of your friend."

"Thank you, Agent. I appreciate that." Hasapi managed a tight smile but he was clearly upset. I hardly blamed him.

What was worse, hearing about the loss of a friend? Or knowing the friend had done something stupid enough to get himself killed?

We retreated, Guzzman leading the way back out. As I walked behind her, observing her gait, I couldn't help but be bothered by her state. She wasn't complaining, but her pain was very obvious to my eyes. To see her move about through willpower and grit was admirable but also not necessary. The urge to do something to help her stirred within me, too strong for me to ignore.

I catalogued which herbs I could see in her greenhouse as we walked back through, a plan forming. I knew some of these and I had a recipe in mind. When we reached the front again, I stalled my two colleagues with an uplifted hand.

"A moment, if you would. I wish to speak with Ms. Guzzman."

Woods didn't care and shrugged, heading back to the car. "Meet you there, then."

Jamie was more curious, but her pad rang at that moment. Lifting it free, she told me, "I'll answer this and meet you at the car."

I waved her on and turned again to address Guzzman. "My dear lady, I don't like leaving you in this state. I'd like to write up a potion remedy that I know works well for rheumatism and gift it to you."

She blinked up at me, head canted in question. "You know enough to do that?"

"I am a royal mage, after all." I winked at her, amused as surprise jerked her head back. She apparently hadn't caught that part earlier. "This recipe I know works well; my grandfather used it for the same ailment. It lasts roughly twenty-four hours and you have most of the herbs you need for it right within your own greenhouse. May I write it down for you?"

"Well." She cleared her throat. "I'm touched at the offer, Royal Mage. Very touched. You Kingston people are kind, aren't you? I'll be glad for the gift."

"Feel free to share it within your community, as well. The recipe for this is common knowledge. The maker of it is so old that it's been lost to the annals of time."

"Good of you, sir. Very good of you. I shall."

I retrieved my notebook from a pocket and wrote it out for her in Itauenese, doing my best to keep my handwriting legible. Then I tore the sheet free and handed it over. "There you go. It brews within an hour and keeps for a year as long as it's stored in a cool, dry place."

"Thank you."

"My pleasure. Have a good day. If you can, give Hasapi the rest of the day off?"

"I plan on it. Man's distraught. Needs time to grieve."

"Very good." I tipped my hat to her and turned, heading for the car.

Jamie leaned up against its side, one leg propped up by the running board, writing notes furiously on the notepad braced against her knee. I could hear Vonderbank clearly as I approached.

"—*can't give us much of a description of the man. She says she only caught a glimpse of him before he hit her with some spell. She swears he was there when she entered and Celto was already tied to the chair and unconscious.*"

"Oh-ho, so he wasn't even aware of things happening?"

"*Apparently not.*"

What was this? Hopeful, I leaned in closer to her pad. "Has Lady Blatt awakened?"

"*Ah, there you are, Davenforth. Indeed, she has, not*

an hour ago. She's drunk some tea and I'm monitoring her state now to see how well that passes. She's a spitfire, this one. She was barely awake before she demanded to see a policeman. Here I thought she'd hardly be able to speak. An amazing woman. She wanted to verify what all had happened and see if the culprit had been caught yet. If she'd had any strength in her limbs, I daresay she'd have lurched out of the bed and gone after the man herself."

"My kind of woman," Jamie commented with a wide smile.

Yes, my darling was much of the same ilk. It was a true trial when Jamie was ill to keep her in bed because of it.

"*She says he was a complete stranger to her.*"

"We'd more or less guessed that was the case." Jamie shrugged. "Still, it's good to know Celto was out for the count when attacked. I can reassure his parents that he really didn't feel a thing when he died, if I speak to them again. We're finding some good leads over here, by the way, so reassure Lady Blatt that we're hot on her attacker's trail."

"*I'll do so. Maybe it will settle her some. By the way, I think I'll leave in the next day or so. Assuming the tea does well in her system, and some porridge this evening, then there's not much more I can do that time alone can't handle. When she's strong enough to leave the bed, I'll portal her home, as any form of travel will be too rigorous for her.*"

He didn't sound at all bothered to still be on guard duty.

There might be some truth to Jamie teasing him about flirting with Lady Blatt's doctor.

"It's good of you, Vonderbank," I acknowledged. "Do keep us updated as to her state."

"*I will. Alright, I'm off, good luck with the investigation.*"

"Thanks." Jamie ended the call, lips pursed thoughtfully. "Well, we knew from evidence there had been a third person there, but it's good to have that confirmed. You think it was the professor himself or a hitman he hired?"

"I've wondered the same, my dear. Depends on how athletic the man is in his old age, I suppose."

"Heh, true. Old doesn't always mean decrepit. I read a story once of a senator who was ambushed by a thief on his walk home from work. It was the thief who ended up in the hospital. The senator was a martial artist, someone who won competitions back in the day, and he still practiced." Jamie straightened, putting the pad away. "Never underestimate old people."

"Truly."

I gave her a hand up into the vehicle, not because she needed it but because I felt strange not offering the courtesy. Besides, it always made her smile. Then I climbed into the backseat with her.

"Officer Woods," I inquired, leaning forward, "might you know where the patent office is?"

"I do, it's practically next door to the station. I figured you'd want to go there next."

"I think it a more viable lead than chasing down the other friend who's on vacation."

Jamie grunted in affirmation. "Me too."

Woods started the engine and turned us about, heading back toward the coastline.

I was grateful for the roof above our heads, as it blocked the chilly winter wind coming in off the ocean. Even in the winter, this place never truly became as cold as Dolivo did. That did not, however, make it warm.

Of course, with the sun like this, I had no doubt the Felixes were sunbathing with delight back at the hotel. Assuming they weren't wandering about with the rest of the group and enjoying the scenery.

Woods had us at the appropriate building with commendable speed even in morning traffic. It was the first building I'd seen in the city that looked like a government building—that is to say, with no personality whatsoever. It was very boxy in shape, shy on windows, with a plain metal door and a sign out front announcing its function. That was it.

Parking being scarce, Woods let us out at the curb and promised to find a place to park further along the street before coming back for us. I waved her on, following Jamie inside the building. Hopefully the employees inside wouldn't mind us requesting their records, otherwise I'd have to fetch Woods back again.

The inside looked much like a library. Rows upon rows of shelves lined the back, all set on massive rollers so they could be shuffled back and forth. A line of plain wooden tables and chairs were arranged along the front. The only thing between us and that section was a very large information desk.

Jamie went directly there and forthrightly asked a clerk, "I'd like to look up a patent."

The clerk blinked at her, then me, before focusing on Jamie once more. The slender brunette reached for a form even as she asked, "What patent? Do you know the maker?"

"I do. Professor Soto was the name given to me, and it was for consumption. I understand it was developed under a grant."

"Your name? I have to record who looked for the records."

"Jamie Edwards."

She wrote it down, the script neat and legible. "Just a moment. I can look that up for you. If you'd like to sit at one of the tables to wait?"

"Yes, please. Thank you."

Well, apparently the office was much like a library. Whoever wanted to look something up could without any fuss.

We went for the nearest table and sat there.

Jamie mused, "What are the odds they'll let us have a copy?"

"I imagine there's some sort of fee involved, but I doubt they'll have issue with it."

"Good. Cause we'll definitely need a copy."

Our clerk returned quickly, a file in hand. She said to us, "It's always so helpful when someone knows the name of the creator. Saves me time. Here's what we have on file for him."

"Thanks so much. Can I get a copy of this before leaving?"

"Of course. There's an administrative fee and a thirty-minute wait."

"That's fine." Jamie accepted the file and promptly handed it to me. "I can't begin to read this, what does it say?"

Our clerk resumed her duties as I opened the file. I knew Jamie was borderline frustrated that she couldn't read anything. For her, I took out my magnifying glass out of my bag and put a translation spell onto its surface so she could read the form. She took it with a smile of thanks and looked over my shoulder.

"A lot of legalese," she noted.

"Indeed."

The connection between this patent and the recipe in production became apparent barely a page in.

"This is definitely it. Filed four years ago, no less. Soto is the only one on the patent."

"First name?" Jamie squinted. "The handwriting is giving me trouble."

"Looks like Rhyse. He was given a grant for it two years ago through the school's funding. Not much of a stipend, but enough to work on it some more. It's identical to what they're making in Dolivo right now. There's no question that Celto copied this."

Jamie just sighed. "Idjut. Alright, anything else of interest?"

I flipped to the next page and my eyebrows shot into my hairline. "Well, well, well. This is a lawsuit."

"Oooh." Jamie leaned in closer, eyes on the page as if she could begin to decipher it upside down. "Do tell."

"It's self-filed, it seems. Only the first part of this is in the right formal language. Filing date was…six months ago." I flipped to the next page, which detailed who had received a copy of the complaint and where. "How interesting. Because it was self-filed, only Celto was given a copy. And the court, of course. This copy came from the court. I don't know if anything came of this. It wasn't filed through international channels. It might well have fizzled out before it could gain any momentum."

"That's just wrong. Not surprising, though, law's like that. If you don't dot the *i*'s and cross the *t*'s, things will get lost in the system. If the man tried to go through legal channels and failed, it would explain why he got frustrated enough to pursue it on his own." Jamie sat back, finger tapping against the polished wood of the table. "If there's no mention of anyone else, then odds are this is our guy. Is there an address listed for Soto?"

"Yes, right at the top." I knew why she asked. "You want to go speak with him today?"

"If we can. I don't want to leap to conclusions. He's still suspect number one, though, and I don't want him slipping through my fingers. It could be that he's innocent. If Celto was ballsy enough to steal the man's formula, there's no saying some other student didn't try the same thing, right? And murdered Celto because he succeeded first."

"An unfortunate theory that might well be right. At the very least, I want to interview Soto. I do give it good odds he was involved somehow."

"I do as well. Alright, let's get a copy of this to take

with us."

I immediately rose, file in hand, to make the request. It was a relief to have a solid lead in this case to give us direction. If our luck continued to hold, we'd find the culprit in short order.

> You jinxed us!
>
> I didn't mean to. It was just an errant thought.
>
> You know better by now. No tempting fate. Now I'll have to perform the appropriate sacrifices to the investigation gods. I wonder what that is...
>
> Paper?
>
> We certainly use copious enough amounts of it.

Report 17: No, Eddy

What with the professor being a prime suspect and all, we didn't leave everyone else to play tourist at the hotel this time. We didn't know what we were walking into, after all. Woods drove up in one vehicle and Henri insisted on driving a second, as one car couldn't take us all.

It's like the man doesn't trust my driving or something.

Don't answer that—I know he doesn't.

Bless all fate for Woods, though. It's not like I could GPS the address, and having someone on hand who knew the city well and could navigate was a relief. She went straight there as if she'd driven to Soto's house a million times already.

It's not like I had a visual in mind for the professor's house and yet when I saw it, it was still somehow exactly what his house should be. A quaint little one-story of brick with a thatched roof, the front yard completely cultivated into a garden of herbs—one that looked sadly overgrown with weeds. It had definitely been neglected for weeks from the looks of it.

Woods pulled us tight up against the curb and people climbed out. I stayed at the little gate leading into the yard, pausing there and waiting for Henri to catch up.

"Jamie." Clint stirred on my shoulder, nose going. "Lots of sniffies."

"Oh yeah?" I looked around too. "Maybe these are all magical plants?"

"They are," Henri confirmed, coming to stand with us. "There's also a very strong ward upon the house."

"You don't say." Now the house looked more interesting

to me. "On a scale of one to ten, one being a deterrent for a robber, ten being a national building, what's this one fall under?"

Henri's eyes narrowed and it wasn't in a good way. That expression meant something wasn't quite adding up for him. "A six."

"Whoa." I didn't expect something that high. "Isn't that a little excessive? Woods, is this area known for crime?"

"Not at all." Her eyebrows stayed arched as she looked the neighborhood over as if with fresh eyes. "This is a very established neighborhood for retirees and such. Crime is practically unheard of."

It didn't make sense to have that kind of ward. Unless you knew that this man had had something precious stolen from him already.

Niamh cleared her throat, catching my attention, and pointed toward the road. "Jamie, something you should be aware of. The same energy signature as the attacker in the factory? It matches what I'm seeing here."

She had my complete attention. "You're sure?"

"Very sure. No mistake." Niamh's eyes were laser focused on the track, not that anyone else here could see it. "I see him leaving perhaps a day ago? No sign of him coming back in."

So he left and really wasn't home? I swung the gate open and headed for the door on the very narrow sidewalk. Three long strides later, I gave the bright blue door a solid knock. Soto might not be home, but that didn't mean no one was.

No answer.

"Rhyse Soto? I'm Jamie Edwards from Kingston. I'm here to talk about your lawsuit?" I figured those words more than anything else would get a reaction.

Still silence.

Could be a very innocent reason for that, but it looked darned suspicious from where I was standing. "You see any sign that anyone else came here?"

"No, none."

"Niamh, can you follow that trail and figure out where

he went?"

"Of course."

Evans lifted a hand. "Let me trail after her with the car."

Smart of him to offer. "Yes, go."

"Well, now, this is a conundrum." Henri's hand indicated the house. "I'd dearly love to get inside. I feel that we'd find many an answer there. However, we've no warrant and no means of crossing through the ward."

Eddy's hand shot up. "I can go in."

"Yes, hon, we know you can," I replied as patiently as possible.

Niamh protested immediately. "Uh, I didn't know he could. For that matter, how?"

Henri turned toward her and explained, "Mr. Jameson in fact has a particular skill set that comes to him as natural as breathing. He has an innate talent that allows him to bypass all wards. It's partially a mindset as well—because he has no ill intent toward the owner, the ward doesn't recognize him as a threat and allows him entry. The two combined makes him impervious to magical barriers."

"Now you see why I insisted on training him as a spy, right?" I shot her a wink.

Niamh stared at Eddy with absolute disbelief. "I'll say. Wait. Wait, you're the kid that kept getting through the palace wards and causing RM Seaton a headache. Aren't you?"

Eddy's chest puffed up with pride. "That's me."

"Oh, now a *lot* more makes sense."

It's funny how this was one of those open secrets among palace staff that she hadn't connected yet. She'd heard the story but not realized it was Eddy somehow. Eddy treating the whole incident like a feather in his cap was funny, too. I noticed Henri wasn't laughing. Still hadn't forgiven Eddy for adding to his grey hairs, eh?

I waved Niamh and Evans on, letting them track down our possible suspect. "Tasha, go with them."

She leapt down and trailed after Niamh. Tasha liked to track people so I indulged her where I could. I had another fish to fry. To Clint and Phil I said, "Take a look around the house if you can. See if anything looks iffy."

The cats were happy to do some investigation and were off like a shot, going opposite directions along the top of the wall. Never mind that the fence width was a mere two inches. Balance issues, what's that?

There were times I seriously envied cats.

Woods lifted a finger to draw my attention. "Edwards, I hate to tell you this, but I don't know if you'd easily get a warrant to search this place. Especially with that ward up because that'll take special effort to bypass."

"I know." The frustration already tugged at me. "I think it's time we made some calls. I need to update my queen anyway."

"Let's retreat to the hotel for now," Henri suggested. "I doubt the Felixes need more than another minute, and there's no reason for us to linger if we can't get in."

"True enough." I mean, I could question the neighbors, but, again, warrant. I could do a lot more with a warrant in hand.

I climbed into the back seat of the car with Henri, letting Eddy take shotgun. Once settled, I pulled my pad out and messaged the queen. I couldn't assume she was available for a chat; the woman's schedule was insane.

I have an update and a request for you if you have a minute.

Hit send and waited.

Clint lightly hopped inside and up to my lap, ears flattened in aggravation. "Lots of sniffies. No way inside. Ward said no."

"I'm not surprised. See anything strange?"

"Just plants," Phil said as he also hopped into my lap.

After all, the reason why I have two legs is for two cats to sit upon them.

Queen Regina called at that moment and I answered promptly. "Hello, hello."

"Jamie, do tell me you're closer to solving this."

"We might well have figured out our perp, actually, but we've hit a snag."

"I'm on the way to a meeting so you have ten minutes to explain."

"Succinct version, then. We found the actual creator of the potion. It was Celto's old Potions professor. The professor had a grant for it and he let students help him with the project. We have both the patent he filed here in Itauen as well as the lawsuit he filed against Celto. He clearly knew Celto had stolen it."

Regina's voice went up several octaves, into the range of screeching cats and train whistles. *"What lawsuit!"*

"Yeah, not surprised you don't know about it; it was self-filed for whatever reason. He didn't hire an international attorney for this and he should have. I don't think the motion got past him sending a copy to Celto. The courts more or less ignored it."

Regina groaned, the sound long and drawn out. *"This is not the update I wanted."*

"I feel you." I did have sympathy for her situation but facts were facts. Only option was to deal with it. "Niamh swears that the professor's aura matches the attacker from the office. The guy's not home—we're sitting outside his house—but she sees a trail leading away from the house and is tracking it now. Thing is, the house has a ward on it that reminds me of Fort Knox— Ah, I mean, it's practically impregnable. I'd need a warrant to overturn it and investigate inside."

Regina paused for a moment and I could almost hear the cogs spinning from here.

"You have motive, clearly."

"Oh, yeah, that in spades. Not sure about probable cause because while he looks suspicious it is also circumstantial at this point. If not for Niamh, I wouldn't be able to say he was at the scene, just that he had motive to kill Celto. Also, the man's retired now. Not sure if he has the physical health to go around attacking people."

Henri leaned in to add, "I might add that the ward around

the house is new. I would put it at three, perhaps four weeks old, and it's built off a much simpler ward that was already in place. He strengthened his security for a reason."

He hadn't mentioned that. It made sense, though, if the professor knew he was going to go murder people and steal his patent back. Of course he'd want to beef up the security at home before leaving. I certainly would have. I wouldn't want anyone inside the house finding clues, like the police.

"*I'll make some phone calls and see if I can get you a warrant expedited. All things told, I can maybe get you one by tonight.*"

Anyone who worked law enforcement could tell you that was blazing fast. Most warrants took a good week to get unless you fast-tracked it by going to the judge yourself for a signature.

"I appreciate it," I responded gratefully. "We'll be on standby. Can you get the warrant to include not only his house and property, but his person as well when we find him? I hope to lay hands on him at some point."

"*Of course. Search and seizure for all three will be included. Sit tight and tell me if you do find him.*"

"Will do." I hung up and blew out a breath. If odds were with us, the man hadn't hopped a ship again. Or a train, or something else that would give Niamh a dead end. "Okay, guess we wait. Woods, can we treat you to an early lunch before you drop us off?"

Woods turned and gave me a smile. "Absolutely. Let's head toward the wharf. Best food is there."

"Wharf sounds good." I hadn't eaten my way through that place yet, but it was not for lack of trying.

We were halfway back to the wharf when my pad rang again. I saw Niamh calling and answered promptly. "Tell me something good."

"*It looks like he got back on a boat before we got here. I've trailed him to the docks. Evans is asking the port master now for records of all the ships that came through here yesterday that took on passengers.*"

Aw rats. Now where did he go?

"Of course he left the country again," Henri muttered darkly. "Of course he did."

What, did he spook or something? Or had he gone out to prove who was really the creator of the potion now that he had the paperwork in hand? Surely he wouldn't be that stupid after murdering Celto.

"Jamie, I feel like an idiot. Why didn't I see his trail at the docks? I should have."

"Hey, don't beat yourself up. There has to be a crazy amount of signatures on those docks, it's a busy place. We think Soto left right after the crew arrived, right? So we just barely missed him. We'll catch up. Okay?"

She still sounded a little irritated with herself. "*Okay*."

"Get that list," I encouraged. "Queen Regina is working on a warrant for us now but we're in waiting mode. We're heading for the wharf if you want to join us there."

"*For lunch? Sounds good to me. We'll meet you there.*"

As I hung up, Eddy turned in the passenger seat and gave the most hopeful, brightest smile ever to grace a human face. "Are you sure I can't go into the house? The ward doesn't bother me a bit."

Primly I answered, "Warrant first."

The poor boy just sighed.

He really acts like I'm depriving him of some treat by not letting him go in there.

He's absolutely incorrigible.

Once he's a spy, there will be absolutely no living with him.

I shudder to think of that future day.

Report 18: Hurry Up and Wait

To my distinct lack of surprise, getting a warrant to investigate on foreign soil was not an expedient process. Queen Regina messaged Jamie and explained it might take a few days to fast-track a warrant. She'd hit more roadblocks than expected and the possibility of gaining it tonight was utterly gone. We were at loose ends until that moment.

The debate on whether to stay here and interview other people who knew Celto, or to return was completely up in the air. There wasn't much to do in either place, frankly. We were waiting on boat records here but they could be forwarded to us. Woods had agreed to do that. Even the interviews here couldn't tell us much that wasn't more concrete than the facts we had in hand. I didn't see the point of sailing once more upwards only to return a few days later, especially when some members of our party suffered from seasickness.

Jamie set Evans, Niamh, and Jameson to search the manifest for Soto's name. I gave it even odds that if Soto really was our culprit, he'd have used a fake name when boarding, just to muddy his trail. But he might not have. He could be on a completely innocent agenda. Either way, the manifest had to be checked.

Jamie and I sequestered ourselves in the lounge area of the hotel, overlooking the ocean, enjoying a quite excellent dessert of fruit cobbler. The cats lounged upon the soft window seat cushions, ears subtly twitching as they caught sounds and dismissed them. Their eyes were closed in contentment. Unless something of the rodent persuasion came by, nothing would tempt them out of their sunbathing.

"Got an update from your dad," Jamie mentioned without any segue. "Business is booming."

"Your strawberry emporium? Business has always been booming."

"It's doubled in profits since last quarter."

I almost choked on my tea. "I beg pardon?"

"Your reaction's a lot politer than mine. I about hit the floor. I asked him how that was even possible and he said demand is now outstripping supply. I mean, they can only grow strawberries so fast, y'know? Magic soil, spells for growth, all of that can only expedite the process so much, and the poor workers are going crazy trying to keep all the crops growing in order to fulfill all the orders."

Oh my. I'd expected, the first time I'd put a strawberry into my mouth, that they would become quite popular. I didn't expect it to balloon this quickly.

Amused, I shook my head. "Well. You, my dear, are about to be a very wealthy woman."

"Between strawberries and my partnership with Ellie, yeah. I'm choosing to reinvest most of it. I asked your dad to set aside a certain amount for us—for a nice down payment on a house—but the rest will either go back into the business or into one of my charities."

Jamie had several that she supported. She mentioned them offhand from time to time. A women's shelter, an affordable housing development, two orphanages, and a scholarship program in a trade school. I was always quite proud of her generosity. She was ever the type to invest in the community around her and we, as a society, benefited from it.

"Your dad's complaining that this isn't what he signed up for. He said I've yanked him out of retirement on false grounds." Jamie snorted, her head shaking in amusement. "I could only laugh. You're the only one who warned us it would grow out of control quickly."

"I did," I agreed equably. "I take it that he's going to hire more managers."

"Said it was the only way he could go home at a decent hour. If I had any kind of head for business, I'd offer to take over, but—"

"Queen Regina would stab you in the foot if she even heard that. You're not allowed to abandon the very department you've founded."

"And there's that. Really, I'm a better investigator. I can't do desk work all day. I'd go crazy."

She was too active of a person for such. It was just as well she understood herself well enough to realize it.

"I'll have to tell my parents about this next time we chat. They'll find this hilarious."

Her scheduled talk with family was coming up soon, in fact. We always gave them a list ahead of time of things Jamie would like—usually books, music, movies, and the like. The medical books I found especially fascinating. Not to mention their botany. It was so alien from ours in many ways and yet incredibly similar. Which, really, only made sense, as Jamie's body chemistry was much the same—distinctly different in some ways and yet remarkably similar in others.

I appreciated beyond measure having new books to read from her world. I had only one complaint. "Seaton and I really must revisit our method of reading off the Kindle. Having to bend over the glass in order to read is difficult on the neck and shoulders for any length of time."

"Yeah, about that, I've been wondering. Is there a reason why you didn't just put that spell on glasses?"

I stared at the love of my life as if her words were just gibberish, sounds without meaning. It felt like the interior of my skull was nothing more than white noise for three full seconds. Then, all at once, her words made sense, and I swore, jerking upright.

"You're telling me that seriously didn't occur to you?" Jamie threw her head back on a laugh. "Seriously?"

I ignored her laughter—justifiable, in this case—and called up Seaton promptly. He answered just as quickly, although he sounded disgruntled.

"*Davenforth, you promised me updates and I haven't heard a blessed word from you.*"

"I'll update you later," I promised him impatiently. "Seaton, we're idiots."

"*A regular occurrence. In regards to...?*"

"Why didn't we just put a translation spell on the glasses for the Kindle?"

Seaton was faster on the uptake than I. He started swearing immediately.

"See? Jamie just asked and for the life of me, I can't fathom why it didn't occur to me."

"*Nor I. Hold on a moment, I have a pair of glasses in the desk somewhere I'm not using—*"

As he rummaged about, I glanced up and found Jamie sipping her tea demurely, golden-brown eyes dancing wickedly with laughter.

"You're going to be insufferable the rest of the day, aren't you?"

"It's not often that I ask a simple question and watch you two in a tizzy. Cheap entertainment is hard to find."

There would be absolutely no living with her after this.

There was an "*Aha!*" of victory and then I heard Seaton designate the spell on the glasses. It felt like seconds oozed by into eternity before he came back, his voice distinct once more.

"*It worked perfectly, of course. Davenforth, why are*

we like this?"

"You two overthink things," Jamie informed him, still grinning. "It's a fault of superbrains, or so I've found. You're welcome, by the way."

"She's insufferably smug, isn't she?"

"Incredibly so. Do make up a pair for Ellie Warner and send them over, won't you? If she finds we have them and she doesn't, there will be consequences."

"Make a pair for me too!" Jamie protested. "There's lots of things I want to read."

I gave her a nod, a silent acknowledgement and promise to do so.

"Our queen as well. I'll make a batch of them, just make my life easier all around. Now, what about my update?"

Jamie's pad rang at that moment and she tilted the screen to show me Vonderbank was calling.

"Sorry, Seaton, must go. I'll call later."

"Promises, promises. Fine."

Jamie answered hers as I hung up.

"Hello, Vonderbank, how are you?"

"Quite well. Lady Blatt is up for talking and wants to speak with you."

"Oh wow, really? Please, put her on." Jamie put the pad on the table and took out her notebook, ready to jot down information.

The voice that came through next was extremely weak, a strained soprano. I couldn't imagine the effort it must have taken to speak. This woman's determination and willpower was admirable in the extreme.

"Agent Edwards?"

"That's me. It's very good to hear your voice, Lady Blatt."

"Thank you. I'm relieved to be alive after all of that. I understand you're investigating. I wish to tell you what I can, although it isn't much."

"Anything you wish to tell me, I'll be happy to hear.

What do you remember of that morning?"

"Everything. I came in for the shareholder reports. I'd arrived the night before, without my maid or escort, but I wasn't worried. The town was peaceful and I was only there overnight anyway. I left early in the morning, after a quick breakfast at the hotel, trying to see Celto before the factory opened for work that day. I didn't like to be in the factory while it was in operation. I felt like all I did was get in people's way."

Understandable. With that many moving parts, a tour of the facilities while it was in operation would be rather crowded.

"The place was quiet and I expected it to be. Nothing seemed wrong or out of place until I made it to Celto's office. When I opened the door, I found him seated behind his desk, but he was unconscious and bound there. I immediately realized the danger and turned to run. I had barely turned before I was hit with something forceful. I was unconscious before I hit the ground."

"You didn't see what or who hit you?"

"Yes and no. I did see who. He was a slender man, perhaps my height or shorter. White hair, tanned skin, he looked to be Itauenian? That's my guess. Much older. I would say near retirement age or just past it. He spoke a spell—I assume it's powerful magic if he could bind Celto as he did."

I didn't have the heart to tell her that Celto was not the magical expert she assumed him to be. However, that description matched with the one we'd been given. If that wasn't Soto, I'd like to know who his doppelgänger was.

"That's very good information." I leaned in to speak more directly into the pad. "We do suspect a man from this country, so your witness statement confirms it."

"You've found a suspect?"

"We have. We're waiting on a warrant before we can proceed. We're making progress on this case, Lady

Blatt. Do not fear there."

"I'm ever so glad to hear it. RM Vonderbank has assured me that in three weeks or so, I might be well enough to travel home and recover there. He's offered to portal me. Will I see you before he does so?"

"Perhaps," Jamie allowed. "If nothing else, we'll need to see you in order to get a written and signed statement from you. For due process, you understand."

"I'd love to meet all of you. My fiancé has nothing but kind words for your entire team. He says you've helped him weather this terrible situation. If you come anywhere near my home, do make time to have dinner with us all."

I saw no harm in that and realized she wanted to give back as she could. "We'd like that very much."

"I'm sorry, I'm tiring quickly. Is there anything else I can help you with?"

Jamie refuted, "Not at this point. I need to speak with Vonderbank again."

"Very well. Good luck."

Vonderbank's stronger voice came on next. *"Yes?"*

"Step out into the hall first, please."

"Alright." A moment later I heard the sound of a door closing. *"Is this sensitive?"*

"Yes, and I didn't want to scare her. What I didn't tell her is that our suspect is currently in the wind. We can't figure out where this guy has gone. That's what the warrant is for."

Vonderbank growled out something that may have been a curse. *"If he realizes that she lived through this..."*

"I know. I know you put a ward up around her room, and I appreciate it, but can you arrange a guard for her before you leave?"

"No. I'll stay until you're back. I won't leave her unguarded against a rogue magician. That's what she's basically facing at this point. The police here won't be

able to thwart this man if he attacks."

No, they wouldn't, and I was glad he realized such. "We have no idea when we'll be back but will alert you when we have a better notion of it."

"*Very well. I'll tell my office back home that I'm delayed.*"

"Thank you. I realize it's putting you out."

"*She's a sweet lady and I won't leave her unguarded here. Rest assured.*"

"Thanks. I'll let you go." Jamie hung up and gave me a speaking look. "An Itauenian, huh? That's nice confirmation to have."

"If she saw him, she can confirm in a court of law that it was him, too. Always a plus."

"Isn't it just."

Jamie's pad lit up with a ring again.

"What is this, Grand Central Station?" she muttered even as she accepted the call. "Hello?"

"*Agent Edwards? This is Egon Durchdenwald.*"

"Hello, Your Highness, what can I do for you?"

"*I've a question for you. Two, really. How goes your demand for a warrant?*"

"Still in process."

"*I feared as such. I've leaned my weight as well through official channels. Hopefully that speeds things up a bit. Now, second question. Is Celto's office still an official crime scene?*"

Jamie looked to me and I shook my head.

"No," I answered clearly. "Frankly, there's no evidence in there that we can further glean from it. Why?"

"*Well, I can't leave the factory without a supervisor for long. We need to put that office to rights for the new supervisor. As sad as I am to lose Celto, I can't let hundreds of thousands of people suffer because we let his work lapse.*"

He apparently hadn't heard yet that this was not

Celto's invention.... I chose not to be the one to tell him. I'd let Queen Regina break that news.

Jamie apparently chose the same, as she didn't remark on it. "Consider the scene released and do as you like. If you don't mind my asking, are you already accepting applicants?"

"*We are. In fact, I have four interviews set up in the next few days.*"

"What are the names? Just for my nosy curiosity."

Jamie never asked a question just for curiosity's sake. I knew she was looking for a certain name in there, one the prince might not question.

"*A moment.*" The rustling of papers. "*Hmm, Dick Vargas, Miles Crawford, Kennedy Snyder, and Dr. R. Toos.*"

"How do you spell that last one?" I had never heard the surname before.

"*T-O-O-S. Rather unusual, not sure where he's from. Or she? I can't tell from just a first initial.*"

"Thank you, Prince Egon."

"*I'll let you go back to work. Keep me updated.*"

Jamie sat back with a sigh, then picked at her dessert once more. "I wish I had work to do. I guess I could go interview more people, but that just makes Woods run around and I'm not sure what else we need to know about Celto at this point except he was a lying liar who lies."

"Truly."

Clint chose that moment to rise from his nap, arching his back in a luxurious stretch before sauntering over to Jamie. He hopped lightly into her lap, rubbing his head against her chest and purring.

"We're in a fine mood after our nap, I see." Jamie rubbed at his head and smiled down at him.

"Good nap," Clint informed her.

"Delighted to hear it. Do you want water?"

"Later. Pets now."

"Oh, I see. There's an order for your needs."

Clint purred and didn't bother to respond.

Having now acquired Phil as a familiar, I was very acquainted with how many demands such a small creature could make. Jamie assured me that this was somehow universal for cats—even while in a different universe. How Jules Felix had managed to create something so like a cat was what boggled the mind.

Clint changed his perch so that his front paws were on the table, back end in her lap, the better to get scratches along his spine. Jamie indulged him even as she finished her dessert.

"Jamie?" Clint was nose to paper with her notebook.

"Yeah, bud."

"This name is funny."

"Which one, Toos?"

"Yeah."

"I agree, kinda an interesting name."

"If you change letters around, it spells Soto."

I once again had a moment where all thought flew out of my mind. I looked sharply down, and even reading upside down, I could see why Clint had made that comment. Indeed, it spelled Soto if you rearranged the letters.

"Jamie. The initial could be Rhyse."

Her eyes flew up to mine. "Get out. Wait, so he just changed his surname around and then went up there to interview for the position?! How ballsy is this man?"

"It makes sense, after a fashion. He knows the potion better than anyone else. If he's supervisor, he can profit off his own work, finally. I admit it seems foolhardy to do so but so is murdering someone for a patent."

Jamie snatched up the pad again. "I'm calling the prince back. This might be our guy. If nothing else, it's worth checking."

"Agreed."

Prince Egon answered promptly. "*Yes, Agent?*"

"Prince Egon, our suspect's name is Soto. Rhyse Soto. That name, Toos, that looks weirdly like an anagram to us. Which country are they from?"

"*Itauen. They were a Professor of Potions at a school there, according to their résumé. You don't think it's him, do you?*"

"It'll be a very strange coincidence if it isn't. That's matching our profile so far. When is their interview?"

"*Tomorrow morning.*"

"Can you move it to afternoon? We're coming up. I want to see this applicant in person."

"*Of course. I'll do so immediately. Do you really think it could be him?*"

"I'd rather not assume but I can't leave it up to chance, either. We'll see you soon."

I was already moving, heading to the napping cats and scooping both up in either hand. If we were to be back in Haverford by tomorrow afternoon, that meant we were sailing overnight and we had no time to waste dallying about here.

Still, even as I moved, I couldn't help but think surely no one would be that stupid.

Surely not.

Report 19: Business is Booming

Bless the yacht captain, he got us ready to go and out of Itauen within three hours of us notifying him we had to move. We made good time, what with the wind spells, and arrived around midnight back in Haverford. We managed to crash at our hotel for some much-needed sleep before we were up and at 'em the next morning.

I counted heads as we got to the dining room, making sure I had all my ducklings. Well, except Niamh. The cats were a given. We were back in cold country so they were warm fuzzy weights in my jacket pockets.

My pad rang and I fished it out, trying to answer it and keep track of people. Ladies and gentlemen, I have recreated the problem of the modern cell phone.

I digressed.

"Yeah?"

"*Jamie,*" Sherard said distinctly, sounding beyond put out, "*first of all, you and Henri STILL forgot to update me.*"

"Oops. My bad. Fire me?"

"*Not on your life. Secondly, we are here.*"

Now he had my full attention. "I'm sorry, who's we and you're where?"

"*Here in Haverford. Queen Regina was beside herself with curiosity so I portaled her up.*"

Knowing my very curious friend, he likely had volunteered to do it. Sherard, I think, was feline in a previous life. Only way to explain his curiosity. But geez, really? Why was it that our queen could never sit still? I wasn't even sure if this was actually the guy! Odds were highly likely, sure, but still.

"Alright, well, we're also here. Where are the interviews happening?"

"*Harbor Street Hotel.*"

"Wait, why there and not the palace?"

"*They're bringing the foremen in for the interview to check technical knowledge before they hire a supervisor.*"

Ahh, so they'd learned from that mistake. That made sense. "On our way."

Niamh sprinted back into the hotel through the front door, spotted me, and dove right for me. She'd said something about looking at the docks before breakfast for a trail and it certainly looked like she'd hit pay dirt. She tugged at my elbow, as excited as a child spotting Santa. "Jamie, he's here! He's back!"

"Our perp?" Oh, lookee here. And it wasn't even Christmas. "Where did he go and how long ago?"

"About one day is my guess and straight into town."

"Follow that. If we split from you at the Harbor Street Hotel, continue to track him. Evans, go with her if that happens."

Evans gave me a casual salute. "Will do."

Now things were shaping up. Even if I was wrong about the Toos guy (I didn't think I was), our perp was in town somewhere. Thank all saints, angels, and pink elephants because really, hunting him down would have been a pain. I had no way of knowing where he'd gone if he hadn't shown up here.

Breakfast was abandoned as we hit the street. We all clustered around Niamh as she led us confidently along the sidewalk.

Niamh ended up leading the way but only until the main street of the town and then she split to the left. She did pause there at the corner and asked, "If I catch up with him, do we apprehend him?"

"Do not engage. This guy's proven to have a temper and is trigger happy with spells. Evans could probably take him but I don't want you or any random passerby in the fallout of that. Just follow, discreetly, and report to me where he is. We'll come up with a game plan of how to trap him."

I really wanted to follow her, honestly, but I was torn. If Toos was the right man, then he was likely near my queen. There was the real chance that the trail Niamh followed might lead directly there. Or it could lead somewhere else. I had no way of knowing. But I wanted to hedge my bets and err on the side of caution, so queen first.

Niamh and Evans went further along the sidewalk and I led Henri, Eddy, and cats into the fancy hotel Lady Blatt had stayed at. I'd barely attained the foyer when the porter recognized me and flagged me down.

"Agent. If you're looking for your party, I can show you the way. They booked two of the adjoining conference rooms."

"That'd be awesome, thanks."

Pleased with himself, he went ahead of me and led us all to the right and toward the back of the hotel. Seriously, I loved this whole town's attitude. They were all invested in catching the bad guy. Made my life easier.

I did scribble a note on my pad to Vonderbank as we moved, just in case.

Perp is back in Haverford. Niamh tracking now. Please do not leave Lady Blatt's side.

The man quickly answered with, *Done.*

I owed him goodies later for being such a good sport.

Two kingsmen in red uniform stood guard at the conference door. I was heartily glad to see both and gave them a smile as I approached. The porter waved me to the door, bowed a little, then retreated the way he'd come, his job done.

"Hello, gentlemen, glad to see you. Anyone else aside from you?"

"No, Agent," the one on the left answered. (His name escaped me just then.) "Just us two. RM Seaton could only portal so many of us up at a time. Prince Egon is supplementing with his own guards."

"Good to hear. Stay on your toes. Niamh has confirmed the perp returned to this town yesterday. She's tracking him now."

They did go more alert at that.

"Can you give us a description?"

"Slender, on the shorter side, tanned skin, white hair, and looks like an Itauenian. Older, retirement age."

"Good to know, Agent. We'll be on the lookout."

"Thank you."

They opened the door for us and we sailed inside. Regina and Sherard were ensconced in comfortable chairs near the fireplace with teacups in hand. Prince Egon paced the window while reading a file in his hands but looked up at my entrance. Even inside here there were guards at the connecting door, standing alert, which reassured me. They were being careful. I mean, Sherard himself could probably take any perp in the world, but I'd rather hedge my bets.

"There you are." Regina sat aside the cup and pointed me toward the empty couch next to her. "Sit, report. I'm sadly out of date."

"Not by much, I promise you." I only paused long enough to catch Eddy's elbow and instruct him, "Go back out get yourself a room and stay there. Read, study, nap, I don't care. I don't want you in the thick of things down here."

He blinked up at me with Sad Face. "But I want to see what happens!"

"No."

Grumbling, he turned and slouched back out.

I had no sympathy to spare for him. I had a pouting queen and she took precedence.

Taking the seat I was pointed to, I let Henri and cats situate themselves as I focused on her. That was to say, all three cats immediately grabbed Khan for playtime. Priorities, after all. "Let me think. My last update to you was?"

"You confirmed that Celto's Potions teacher had filed a case against him and were trying to get into the man's house but couldn't."

"Ah, right." We were still waiting on that warrant, too, but that was neither here nor there. "Sadly, that means you're mostly updated. The only thing I can add is that Niamh picked up the perp's trail on the way here. She's tracking it now."

"Did it approach this hotel?" Egon demanded, striding over to join us.

"Trail she picked up was from yesterday and headed further up the street. No telling where he is at this moment."

Henri leaned in toward Sherard. "If Niamh catches up with him, she's instructed to report it to us immediately. I'd prefer if we both portal to her to catch him. I do not wish to risk anything or anyone for lack of precaution on our part."

Sherard was always happy to go tackle the bad guy. He perked up like a dog with a new bone to chew. "Absolutely, count me in."

I felt like two royal mages was overkill, but I wasn't about to tell one of them to stay and chill either. One of them would be mad at me and it just wasn't worth the argument.

Prince Egon at least looked perturbed by this. "If you hadn't said something, we might well have welcomed the murderer right into our midst without suspecting a thing."

Regina tilted her head up, catching his hand with hers and giving him a smile. "And this is why I wanted her on the case to begin with."

"Yes, I see now. Agent Edwards, is it safe enough to do the interviews I have lined up already? I have two people waiting on me now for interviews."

I didn't see why not. "Of course, go ahead. Uh, maybe take either Henri or Sherard with you just in case. If nothing else, they can tell you from a magical expert's perspective if the person actually has the skills or is full of hot air."

Prince Egon looked pained. "Yes, clearly I'm not a good judge of that. RM Davenforth, would you mind accompanying me?"

"Not at all, Your Highness." Henri rose immediately and followed him through to the adjoining room.

Henri was a good choice for that. The man had done

so many interviews trying to get a magical examiner in with the police that he was an interviewing expert at this point. Egon probably invited him just because he's mild-mannered though.

Regina turned to orient herself, facing me directly. "I am highly looking forward to our Girls' Night. It is much needed."

"Same. We have certainly earned it."

Sherard whined, "Can't I be a girl and come to one of these?"

His queen pointed a stern finger at him. "No."

Muttering, he looked off toward the fire and drank his tea.

The door abruptly opened and Niamh hurried through, her eyes a little wide.

I knew that look. Crap was about to hit the fan. I was out of my seat without thinking.

"What? Where is he?"

"Back here somewhere, I think in the other room or somewhere near there. I got blocked from going further."

"How recent?"

"Past hour, at most."

Aw, cripes. I really should have listened to instinct and gone with her. Well, maybe not. This way, at least, Henri was with Prince Egon and Sherard was cued up. Maybe I had been smart to come directly here after all.

"Show me. Evans?"

"Waiting in the hallway just in case he shows up."

I was out the door in a blink, right on her heels. She was right that the door at the end of the hallway was blocked, but it was by a secretary with a makeshift table, clipboard, and a guard at the door. Evans was already arguing with the secretary, although he kept his voice low.

"—suspect we're chasing. Let us pass."

"I assure you, sir, no unsavory types have passed this point. You're mistaken."

Oh, I'd have words with this one later. In the meantime,

I just pulled my badge and waved it in her face. "Let us pass."

Her mouth tightened mutinously before she opened it, ready to retort.

I didn't give her any more attention. I went straight for the door and when the guard tried to block me, I repeated it for him.

"Agent Edwards with Queen Regina. Let me pass."

He blinked at the badge, recognized it enough to give me a nod, and moved out of the way.

He would get a cookie. The mean lady would not.

The room beyond the door was another conference room, only large enough for a single table, eight chairs, and a sideboard lurking in one corner. They were using it now as a waiting room for the interviewees. Two were seated there, with the width of the table between them, clearly not interested in chatting with each other.

I never had understood that, as I would talk to absolutely anyone in the room with me. But I'm an extrovert.

One of them was an elf, by the look of it, dressed in a neat suit and her hair up in a braided bun at the top of her head. She regarded us with quizzical curiosity but no alarm.

The other guy rang alarm bells for me immediately. Short, slender build, tanned skin, white hair cropped close, looked to be in upper seventies. I didn't need Niamh's hiss behind me to know this was the guy. She was both alarmed and vindicated to finally find her quarry.

Sometimes, the direct approach was the best. I looked straight at him and his eyes widened. I think, in that moment, he knew. Jig was up.

"Rhyse Soto?"

I expected a response. I didn't expect him to throw himself out of his chair, snatch a wand out of his pocket, and hurl a spell at the nearest window. It broke without resistance, the sound loud as the concussive force of both magic and glass shards flew all over the place.

I ducked down, rolling toward the table in an effort to find some cover. Why I did that, I had no idea, because none of it could have hurt me. Survival instincts got me.

When I popped back up, he was gone, having disappeared through the window.

"Well," I said to no one in particular as I scrambled up to my feet. "I guess that answered that question. Niamh, Evans, let's go!"

They weren't even waiting on me, already running for the window.

The connecting door burst open and Henri's head popped around the doorframe.

"Dearest, what was that noise?!"

"Our perp just exploded a window and went through it." I didn't mean to sound excited about that. I just liked a good chase scene. "Time to run, Henri. The game's afoot."

Awww, Henri, you wouldn't chase him with me!

You had Niamh and Evans to run with. No.

spoilsport

Report 20: Seaton Ran for Me

lolol I love how that was the important thing for you
#truefriendship #truefriendsrun

Seaton was halfway into the room, looking for the sound of the noise and ready to give chase, only to jerk himself to a stop. His expression said all—he abruptly remembered he had a monarch to protect. Two, technically, as we were the only royal mages present. Prince Egon had only a small retinue.

While it was my job to chase after the suspect, I had no desire to exert myself in such a manner. Besides, Seaton was longer of limb and quicker of pace. I could tag him in, as Jamie would put it, and let us both play to our strengths.

A fine justification, even if I did say so myself.

I caught his eye with a wave of the hand. "I'll protect them. Go."

He bounced off, like an eager puppy that had escaped its leash.

Upon entering the room, Queen Regina eyed me in that knowing way females had, silently declaring she knew what I truly thought. I smiled back at her, not denying it. Why run when I had excellent colleagues who were eager to do so?

No one was willing to just sit and wait, however, so we all went to the windows to catch any glimpse we could of the events outside. The Felixes were right beside us, just as eager to see. I did take the precaution of putting a warding spell on the glass to prevent anything from breaking through, but it only took a moment.

In that moment of inattention, a great deal happened.

Niamh, Woodland Elf that she was, could far outstrip most humans in a chase scene. Only Jamie could keep up with her. She had tackled our perpetrator—or tried—but he dodged her somehow and kept his feet.

I could see his magic flare to life like an aura around his body. It was strong, a sharp rendition of energy, the likes of which I rarely saw. This man had retired as a potion's master? With *that* kind of magical ability?

I hadn't questioned what he'd done earlier in his life, and, in retrospect, that was a significant oversight.

Evans threw up a blocking barrier around the yard at the back of the hotel, caging him in, which was smart. It kept people from accidentally wandering in, as well as protecting the area. Evans no doubt saw what I had. This man was not someone who could be easily taken down.

Jamie was circling to the side, looking for an angle. Seaton caught up in that moment. For once, I was slightly worried about her coming up against a magician. Normally, I didn't—she was immune to any offensive spell. But a man of *this* caliber might well figure out her weaknesses if he engaged with her for any length of time.

Soto faced them all with his knees slightly bent, magic at the ready. We'd wondered if he hadn't hired a hitman somehow, considering how old he was, but looking at him I knew that wasn't the case. He was a strong individual, still light of foot, and the way he stood made me think he'd received a fighter's training at some point. Jamie stood like that when she faced an opponent. He was incredibly lithe for someone of his age. In fact, I knew people decades younger that would struggle to keep up with him.

No, he'd had the strength and dexterity to do his own dirty work.

"How did you know?" he demanded, voice rising in outrage. "How did you know it was me?!"

"You're not as smooth as you thought," Jamie called calmly.

She was in that stance, the one where she offered only a profile to her opponent, weight on her toes, ready to burst forward the second she saw an opening. I'd seen her like this many a time. Few survived first contact.

"I left no trace!" Soto insisted on a snarl, miffed beyond anything.

Niamh waved fingers at him in a truly condescending manner. "Woodland Elf here. You left a clear trail there and back again, thanks very much."

He stared at her for a full second before swearing viciously. "Is that how?"

"One of our clues, yes." Jamie approached two steps, but they were almost sideways more than forward. Changing angle of attack? "Soto, you're way outnumbered. You're good, I grant you, very good. But the man at my side is a royal mage from Kingston. There's another royal mage just inside. Don't you think it's better to just stand down?"

He twitched at that. His eyes flew to Seaton, standing still and ready at Jamie's side, and made his own evaluation. I didn't need to be a mind reader to see what he thought. He was unnerved by Seaton's presence. Really, anyone with common sense would have been.

Soto swallowed his first response and visibly reworded it. "You've no right to stop me like this. Celto *stole* it from me. I had every right to take it back!"

"You had every right," Jamie agreed. "But guess which is worse according to the law? Theft or murder?"

"HE STOLE IT FROM ME!" Soto bent under the force of his scream, the words echoing under the force of the magic barrier around him.

I did feel some sympathy for him. He'd tried, in his own way, to pursue this legally. If he'd hired the right lawyer, it might have gotten somewhere. He might have been able to reclaim his own creation without coming away with blood on his hands. He'd either been too upset or too impatient to try again. Soto had jumped straight to brute force.

My sympathy had limits.

"We know Celto stole it from you," Jamie responded patiently. "We know he did. I have a copy of your suit against him. Prince Egon and Queen Regina have both seen it. We're in no doubt you're the creator, alright?"

That mollified him some. But he was intelligent enough to know this didn't mean he was absolved from the crimes he'd committed.

"You've two members of royalty here. If they really do believe I'm the creator, then let me go. I'm not to be held responsible for their deaths."

Jamie didn't correct his assumption that Lady Blatt had died. "Uh, sir, you threw bombs into two people's chests. No one can overlook that. Taking the patent back is forgivable, but murder's way crossing the line. How about you come in and pitch your case, though? Maybe they can find some leniency for you."

Soto didn't seem to find good odds in that. He swore, shaking his head.

No good, Jamie. Reasoning with him would do no good. I didn't fault her for trying. It would be easier if he just surrendered instead of battling him to a standstill.

Prince Egon stirred at my side. "Would it help if I spoke to him, promised him something?"

Queen Regina patted his arm. "It's fine, my darling, Seaton has this."

So he did. I could see the magical buildup in my friend a split second before he spoke the spell.

"*Infercino*," he said distinctly, and fire burst from

his hands toward Soto.

Soto did not flinch at the two pillars of flame shooting directly at his body. He tucked and rolled, coming up lightly to his feet. He threw out his own attack, slicing a large chunk of grass and dirt off the top of the ground before throwing turf like a scythe through the air.

Jamie and Seaton both rolled off to the side, avoiding it. Evans, smart man, threw up a shield in front of himself and Niamh. Elves had no defense against magic like this, not inherently, and she was in danger if something did manage to hit her.

Seaton rolled up to one knee, arms coming over his head as he drew on the ambient power all around him, sharpening and honing it into another spell. He used the same amount of energy and power, no more, still testing his opponent's defenses.

"*Coercere.*"

Soto deflected the immobilization spell with an upward strike of his palm, his magic enough to make the poles of air go over his head and impact harmlessly against Evans' shield.

Gun in hand, Jamie aimed low firing a short series of shots at Soto's feet.

Soto ran ahead of her aim, avoiding the bullets as they bit into the dirt. The reports of the gun echoed through the air, overlapping. Soto did not advance, however; as soon as he reached the limits of the building, he turned sharply like a dancer, darting back the way he had come, careful to keep distance between them.

I saw the spell build in his wand, quick and hot, and swore. Before I could get a warning out, Soto hurled the same bomb spell he'd used against Celto and Lady Blatt, firing it at Jamie and Evans.

Evans blocked, but at a cost. The bomb exploded against his shield and went upward. Niamh was knocked off her feet, and the explosion threw both Evans and Jamie back, Evans falling flat on his back. Jamie just barely kept her balance, and my heart was in my throat watching her. Very few things could knock her so off-balance and if she fell now, the others would be in danger. She was immune to spells, she could hold the line, but the others were more vulnerable.

Even though I knew the danger for her was minimal, I still shook with the urge to fight at her side. If not for duty holding me in place, I would have been through that window in an instant.

Even as my thoughts raced, she was quick to get her gun up again to fire. My heart only barely settled seeing her up and moving; she had clearly taken no serious damage from the blow.

Seaton threw his own ward up around Niamh and Evans, protecting them, giving them a moment to find their feet. I hoped they would, at least. I hoped they'd only been thrown back and not injured.

Our perpetrator was running once more, using a shield to deflect bullets, and he was giving Jamie serious trouble. The man was entirely too wily and hard to cage. I never thought he'd give three trained professionals and a royal mage this much trouble.

Would they be able to subdue him before someone sustained serious injury?

If not for the two monarchs I'd promised to protect, I'd have dived into the fray already. I felt distinctly on edge, restless with the desire to move.

"What is Seaton doing?" Queen Regina demanded in aggravation. "He's just kneeling there and letting Jamie do all the work."

I'd been so distracted with Jamie's efforts I hadn't paid attention to Seaton. At my queen's remark, I glanced his direction and realized in a second flat what those two were doing.

"Oh, clever," I murmured in admiration. "Now

when did they have time to plan that?"

My queen grabbed my arm and shook me lightly. "Don't say cryptic things like that. What are they doing!"

"Bait and trap, in essence."

I hardly had time to explain as they were on the verge of springing it. Jamie's bullets were both distraction and herding. She was guiding Soto back into a specific spot and simultaneously making sure he didn't look too carefully at where he was going.

Seaton, on the other hand, had put a binding spell into the grass itself, turning the blades into binding ropes. Such a clever man, my friend. If I hadn't known him well and was looking for the catch, I wouldn't have seen it.

Soto's foot grazed the grass, his toe just at the edge of the spell. So close, he was almost inside the—

—He just did a backflip. In the air.

Great dark magic, just how flexible was this man?! Even Jamie would struggle to move as he did, and she was magically enhanced!

Soto flipped lightly through the air, finding his feet as naturally as a Felix would after leaping off a ledge. I was absolutely speechless at this display. Truly, what kind of training had this man done in his life to move like this?

He changed tactics, switching from defense to offense. Keeping his torso low to the ground, he bent forward and charged, magic flaring into his hands.

No. No, you do not get to cause any more trouble.

My eyebrow twitching in aggravation, I lifted my own hand and cast through the window, my words crisp and cutting. "*Pulstro.*"

Like a blunt hammer to the chest, my spell caught Soto completely off guard. It snatched him up into thin air, throwing him sharply backward into the very trap he'd just evaded. Seaton's spell was still active and it snatched its prey eagerly, the grass wrapping around him from head to toe. It held him tightly to the ground without any wiggle room available.

"Nice, Henri!" Jamie called, waving a hand. "Such a good follow-up."

"I do try," I responded, winking at her in return.

Regina put a hand over her chest as she blew out a relieved breath. "That was more of a fight than I expected. He's incredibly skilled."

"Indeed. It's no wonder he caught Celto and Lady Blatt so unawares." I didn't dare relax until Soto had magical restraints put on him. I didn't trust that man.

Evans went to check on Niamh, who was already standing and brushing off her pants. She was fine, it seemed. I was relieved to see them both on their feet. Satisfied, Evans turned his attention to their surroundings and started the repair work for the damaged lawn on behalf of our host.

Always thoughtful, was Evans.

"Come along, Sushi-Perp," Jamie singsonged, skipping to Soto. "It's my favorite time of the day. Interrogation time! You will be our celebrity for the event."

Oh, she was definitely in a good mood now.

"Sushi-Perp?" Prince Egon repeated blankly.

"We'll have Jamie prepare some sushi so you can try it," Queen Regina promised him. "She says she's not as good as a professional chef but I quite enjoyed it when she made it last time."

"Respectfully, Your Majesty, her pizza is better," I tacked on.

"Oh? What is that, pray tell?"

"If we can borrow the hotel's kitchen, I have no doubt she'll make us some in celebration."

My good queen was always up for something delectable and new, much like myself. She smiled and nodded. "I'll ask her. First, however, I want answers

from that man."
   Yes indeed. I had a few questions myself.

Report 21: Oldest Motive in the Book

Haverford Police Station hosted us for the interrogation and holding process. No other place to put Soto, really. Henri had apparently anticipated the need for this because he whipped out some magical restraints that turned Soto from a deadly magician to a frisky old man. I preferred the frisky old man. Him I could handle.

The fight had more or less gone out of him. Or at least, he didn't physically struggle when we dragged him to the station. He kept glaring at everyone like he couldn't believe this had happened.

My dude, you killed a person and tried to kill another. What did you honestly think would happen?

I got brownie points for not saying that out loud.

We parked Soto inside the room, left Evans to guard him for a moment, then stepped out again. I had a due process question to answer before we could get going, and only the royalty could answer it for me.

International law was still a huge question mark in my brain. It's why I had a Gibs.

In the adjoining room, separated by a two-way mirror, sat the royalty. I directed my question to my queen, as that felt most appropriate.

"Before I begin, where exactly is he going to be tried? I don't know what kind of paperwork to do or where to send him after we get our answers."

Regina glanced at her boy toy. "It might have to be Itauen."

"Indeed, I was about to say the same. They've been quite

upset that one of theirs has caused trouble on foreign soil. They want first stab at him."

The way he said this made me think the stabbing thing was not a metaphor.

Um, well, that only half answered my question. "I don't know how they process people in Itauen though. We're still technically waiting on a warrant."

"I do," Prince Egon assured me. "I have a solicitor standing by who will handle the paperwork for us. With his attack near Our presence, it trumps all other due process. We are free to question and detain him. All I need from you is a record of the interrogation and all the evidence. Any notes you made during the case as well would be beneficial. They will quite likely call you up to Itauen to testify against him at some point, but we can discuss that at a future date."

Wait, hold up. I got to close a case *and* skip the paperwork? Wow. It wasn't even my birthday yet!

I'd take the win. Not looking this gift horse in the mouth, no siree.

I beamed at him. "Fine by me. Before I go in there, any specific questions you want answered?"

"I want to know why he attacked Lady Blatt." Regina's teeth audibly ground together. "I do not understand that at all as she wasn't involved in the theft of the potion."

"It's a good question that I've wondered myself. Prince Egon?"

"I want to know if he planned to reveal himself as the true creator."

Also a good question. It would have been stupid to do so, in my opinion.

"A personal question, if I may." Egon looked at Henri directly, head canted in question. "Why did you switch with RM Seaton and have him give chase as you did? I found that whole exchange odd."

To anyone who didn't know these two, it likely would have been.

"Two reasons, Your Highness." Henri held up two fingers,

expression so bland as to be dry. "First, RM Seaton is more magically powerful than I and regularly duels. He's the more combat ready."

Henri, dearest, you take down criminals with spells often. I doubt you're less combat ready.

"Secondly,"—the tone went oh so dry—"I am as swift as a Felix. An old one. With arthritis. Run over by a car eight days ago."

Regina snorted a laugh behind her hand.

"When it comes to running, I don't have a prayer of keeping up with her,"—Henri inclined his head toward me—"and Seaton, for some reason, loves the challenge of a chase. If there is running to be done, I'll let him do it."

Prince Egon was clearly laughing on the inside. "I see. I'm surprised, considering you were a policeman."

"I was a magical examiner until Jamie decided she liked me. My days of safe lab work ended at that point."

He said that but I knew he didn't regret it. I gave him a challenge. Henri liked thinking outside the box.

I rubbed my hands together. "Any other questions? No? Okay, good. Cats, stay in here, please."

Regina had Khan with her, so my cats practically leapt out of my pockets so they could play with him. Traitors. I let it go. They were cute but not helpful in interrogations.

Henri followed me into the other room, readying a black box as he did so. Evans didn't leave, just in case. None of us trusted this man. He was definitely more than met the eye.

Soto watched the preparations with a mix of anger and resignation. There was no cunning in his expression like he had a plan of how to get out of this. Which is just as well because he really couldn't.

Not with the incriminating evidence he had carried into the interview.

I took the chair across from Soto, letting Henri work the box, and focused on my criminal.

"Well, sir, you took us on quite the trip around the world. I've visited countries I've never seen before because of you. Allow me to introduce myself. I'm Queen's Agent Jamie Edwards, of the Queen's Own in Kingston. I represent Queen Regina's interests here. Prince Egon's too. This is my partner, Royal Mage Henri Davenforth, and our colleague, Queen's Agent Evans. For the record, can you state your full name and address, please."

He pried open his mouth to answer but the man's eyes were lasers. Lasers, I tell you. I should have melted like a James Bond girl.

"Rhyse Soto, House 46 on Cliff Terrace, Itauen."

"Thank you. Well, where shall we start? How did you know the deceased, Mattius Celto?"

"He was a former student of mine. The worst traitorous eel that I'd ever met. The dean of the school didn't like for anyone to flunk, so he asked me to give the man some kind of project to help his grade. I thought he could handle the manual labor that came along with potion brewing so I agreed." Soto rolled his eyes expressively. "I should not have. He wasn't up to the task. Celto was one of those who was so far behind he thought he was first."

"I know the type. It was then that he came across your consumption cure, I take it?"

"Yes. That was my second mistake, not that I knew it then. I was so incredibly close to finalizing the potion, of making it perfectly effective. When we'd started it that semester I had just been given a grant for its research. I'd tested it some on animals and, while it did work, it took a series of dosages and not every animal survived long enough to benefit from the full regime. It was frustrating to see progress but not have the time to really dig into the problem. That's why I brought the students into it. With them doing the shopping and manual labor for me, we saved an incredible amount of time. The grant, too, covered the costs for the more expensive ingredients."

It was like talking to a scientist. A frustrated one. "I did wonder why you changed to foreign herbs. They're more expensive, as you said."

"The efficacy of the herbs grown locally wasn't potent enough."

Henri cleared his throat a little before chiming in. "I took a look at the potion you'd used to gain the grant. The *Hydherba* alone was less effective than the *Rubilium* that you substituted it for. The herbs grown in colder climates have a stronger potency than anything tropical."

Soto turned to him as if suddenly fascinated. "You understand herbology. Royal mages study that?"

"I was a magical examiner, once. It came along with the job."

"Oh." Soto's lips curved in a smile. He liked that someone at the table understood his science. "Yes, that was the stumbling block I had. I didn't want to use foreign herbs, of course; it drove the costs up. I didn't think of approaching a different country to make the potion in. Celto was ingenious in that, at least. Or desperate enough to put distance between us after he stole my potion to try it."

"Likely a matter of both. When did you discover he had stolen it?"

"Not for a good year after I had him that semester. It wasn't until a colleague in Dolivo wrote to me, excited because someone had broken through the barrier of curing consumption, that I suspected anything. He and I have corresponded for years regarding the potion. Indeed, he was the one who suggested *Rubilium*, *Proscinem*, and *Virigus* to me. Brilliant man, truly brilliant. I asked him who the creator was and, to my astonishment, he named Celto! I told him he was quite mistaken, I knew the man, and he was a dunce with potions. But he clipped out a newspaper article and sent it to me as proof. That's when I knew. That traitorous, pond-sucking lowlife had stolen my creation for his own."

Rage was back with a vengeance. Any hotter and steam would be coming out of the man's ears. He was literally red in the face.

"Then what?" I prompted.

"I filed a suit against him, of course. It didn't do any

good. I don't know why. I kept waiting and waiting for the court to contact me with a trial date but heard nothing but silence."

Oh dear. Oh my. This poor idiot. Smart as he was with potions, he didn't seem to understand anything about law and how it worked.

I thought about being gentle, but I liked myself all feisty, so I just spat it out. "You filed a suit without a lawyer and without doing anything more than sending a copy of it to Celto. Of course it didn't go anywhere. The lawyers are the ones who set up court dates and get a trial prepped for hearing."

He looked at me as if I spoke nonsense. "But I filed with the court."

"You didn't set anyone up as representative. You didn't go back to the court and set a date for trial even as a self-representative. Just filing a suit doesn't do anything unless you pursue it."

Soto looked like I'd just taken a clue-by-four and smacked him in the back of the head with it. Really? He didn't think to question why his case hadn't gone anywhere? He didn't go back to the court and ask questions? My goodness, lordy, someone help this poor idiot.

Well, what he should have done was a moot point anyway. I moved us along.

"Alright, so suing Celto didn't work for you. What next?"

"I decided to take matters into my own hands if the law wouldn't help me." Soto stared at his hands, expression bewildered now. No doubt wondering what might have been if he'd stopped and thought about it all. "I wasn't about to let years of work be wasted on that dunderhead who couldn't even brew the potion. I came up with a plan. I'd go to him, demand he reveal the truth. I had the grant paperwork with me to prove this was mine and not his. With his testimony, I could overturn his position there and gain the backing I rightfully deserved."

He took in a breath, anger resurfacing, but his eyes never

lifted from his hands. Too locked up in memory, perhaps.

"I took a ship to Haverford. It wasn't hard to find him—everyone knew where he was. He was a local hero, after all. Oh, how it galled to hear people speak of him like that. I met him at the factory and spoke with him. He had the audacity to first be surprised that I knew, and then—"

Soto paused, breathing hard, his hands tightening together until the knuckles shone white.

"—and then he had the audacity to plead I leave things alone. To just let him be the face of it all. He offered me fifty percent of the proceeds. *Fifty percent.* Like he'd earned any of that at all!"

Really glad for the magical cuffs by now. He'd have torn this room apart without that suppressor in place. As it was, Henri had edged ever so closer to me, hand under the table in a position he only used when he was about to cast. Soto unnerved him and he was ready to throw a spell at the man and hustle me down to the floor before the table could fly.

"I couldn't believe my ears. Couldn't believe the sheer audacity he had. His greed made him think he could hoodwink me even further. I'd had enough at that point. I left because talking didn't do any good. I left, and I paced around the factory, and I thought. I watched him for days, not able to eat or sleep, just knowing he had to pay for what he'd done. It was then that I saw an opening. He always came in early to the factory, a good half hour before the rest of the workers. Funny, as he was always late as a student. No doubt an effort he made to look more responsible, but it gave me the opening I needed."

Soto finally lifted his head and this time spoke directly to me. There was no shame in his expression, no regret, just remembered hatred. "I ambushed him in his office that morning. I bound him to the chair he sat in, demanded to know where the patent was. He wouldn't tell me, just kept insisting we could use the situation to our benefit. I stopped listening to his gibberish, did a seeking spell, and found it on my own."

He had to pause again, swallowing several times.

"I'd learned in the army how to create small bombs. We used them for construction work, mainly, but I couldn't think of a more painful death for him. I wanted him to hurt. I was about to cast the spell when I heard someone coming up the stairs. It was his woman, there to meet with him, and I didn't expect her at all, hadn't seen any sign of her before this. I panicked a little. I knocked her out, bound her as well, but she'd seen me. I was sure she'd seen me. I had to kill her too to cover my tracks. Not much loss, really. Anyone in cahoots with Celto deserved to lie in the bed of their making."

I'd correct him in a minute. He was on a roll now; best to let him keep talking.

"I had everything out of the office I needed to prove the potion mine. I attached a bomb spell to each of them and timed them so I could be out of the building before they went off, just a ten-minute delay. It gave me the chance to remove their bindings, write a suicide note to explain their deaths. Then I left. There was nothing more I could do, and it was best I wasn't in town when the deaths went under investigation. I went home to pack and prepare my next step. If Celto, as limited as he was in qualifications, could get an interview for this position of factory supervisor, I knew I could. I just had to get an audience with the prince. Then I could reveal all."

I pulled the briefcase he had a little closer and fished out a few things, careful to handle them with gloves on. "That's why you had a copy of your grant, the lawsuit, and the stolen patent on you?"

"Yes." Soto stared at me defiantly.

Did he not get that the stolen patent was the final nail in the coffin that linked him to the crime scene?

Aw man. He really didn't understand law.

Henri was nicer than me. He explained things. "The suicide note was the first thing that tipped us off, actually. The spell you used to fake Celto's handwriting was noticeable."

Soto twitched. He stared at Henri in dismay. "You

discovered that?"

"Magical examiner, remember? I check for things like that. Also, you made an assumption you should not have. The woman there was not Celto's lover. She is Lady Blatt, an investor. She was there to gather the shareholder reports."

"Not...his lover?"

"No, indeed. She's quite cross with you, in fact."

"Wait, you're speaking of her in the present tense. She didn't die?"

"She did not," I confirmed cheerfully. "She had a charm on her that deflected most of your bomb. Due to her own tenacity and some excellent medical care, she pulled through and will make a full recovery. So you only murdered one person."

He didn't seem to know what to think of this. "She survived?"

"If at first you don't succeed, it's only attempted murder."

Henri poked me in the ribs for my wisecrack.

Look, I can't help myself. The lack of paperwork after this made me a little giddy, so sue me.

Henri stepped in to be the responsible one.

"Rhyse Soto, you'll be tried for the murder of Mattius Celto, the attempted murder of Lady Blatt, and the purposeful destruction of property. You'll be notified once it's decided where you'll be tried but, for now, you'll be held here. Is there anything else you wish to say?"

Soto looked pleadingly to him. "I'll be named the creator after this, won't I? My potion will still be made?"

"Yes, it will be made. Celto's name will be removed from the potion entirely."

That satisfied him. He sat back with a smile. "Good. Good. Then I am content."

Wow. Let's talk priorities here, man. 'Cause yours are messed up.

I shook my head and stood, taking Soto's bag with me. Once we were in the safety of the hallway I just looked at Henri, at a loss for words.

"He's not even worried about the woman he almost wrongfully killed." Henri rubbed at his forehead. "In his position, I would be."

"In his position, I'd be worried about a lot of things. Well, anyway, that's a wrap. Let's tag some evidence and get people on their way home. I, for one, am missing my own bed."

Henri's a homebody so he was all over this idea. I'd never seen him move that fast.

We packed off royalty, Sherard taking home Regina and kingsmen, Egon going off with his retainers. I bagged and tagged the last of the evidence that was on Soto's person and requested his hotel room be cleared by the local cops and anything in it brought here, also to be retained for evidence. An hour's work was all it took for us to sort out the details and then it was off to the hotel.

Henri went to find the ship captain to ask if the yacht could take us home today. Otherwise we'd stay another night and ship out tomorrow. I was okay either way, honestly. I got to put my feet up and read, which was reward enough after a hard case.

That left me with just Eddy as we walked back to the hotel. Well, him and cats, as Evans and Niamh stayed guard over Soto until Egon's magicians could come in and take over.

"How was it, your first case?" I asked my trainee.

Eddy had a bounce in his stride, a grin splitting his face ear to ear. "It was great! So exciting. Do your cases always have chases?"

"No. Fortunately for Henri."

"What about explosions?"

"Not those very often either, fortunately. Messes up evidence, you understand."

"Will I solve cases as a spy?"

"No, but you'll need to gather the right evidence to bring back, hence I'm training you as an investigator."

"Oh, okay." He walked along for another beat before asking, "So when should I give it back?"

Alarm bells started ringing in the back of my head. "Give what back, kiddo?"

"Seaton's wallet. When should I give it back?"

I stopped dead, my jaw dropping so hard it hit the other side of the planet. "When did you pickpocket him?!"

"A while ago. At the hotel." Eddy blinked up at me with wide, innocent eyes. "He's not safe to practice on?"

Guys. Guys, help. I think I created a monster.

Sherard: Jamie, I had to portal *back* for my wallet. Do you know how embarrassing that was?

Jamie: Henri can still top you.

Henri: This isn't a competition, and please talk sense into that child. Before he does something incredibly stupid, like rob a prince.

Jamie: I promise you, limits have been set.

Henri: Praise heaven.

Final Report: Piizzaaaaaa
Happy birthday to me, ♪♪ ♫ ♪♪ happy birthday to meeeeeeeee

I chose to hold my thirtieth birthday on castle grounds. Not anywhere fancy in the buildings, just in the grassy courtyard area between the Queen's Own building and the Kingsman's Offices. We did have to attach heating charms and set braziers in with the tents to keep the winter chill at bay, but I did it mainly for strategic reasons.

Pizza reasons.

I had, of course, made pizza quite a few times while living on this world. Henri adored it. Ellie made me fun inventions for the promise of two full pizzas. We're not even going to talk about what Gibs would do for a slice. But despite my growing fanbase, I had clearly not corrupted the right people yet, as there was still a distinct lack of pizza parlors in this city.

This was my bad. I would correct it.

First, to introduce it to the masses. I was not above using my own birthday party to spread corruption.

I had a build-your-own-pizza station on one table, another table full of already baked pizzas so people could try it first. Those who already knew what pizza was went immediately for the build-your-own table and loaded up. Hearing Henri and Sherard debate on what was best on pizza, and what was disgusting and why would you do that, almost brought a tear to the eye. It was too reminiscent of similar discussions at home.

"There's the birthday girl!"

I turned at the hail and smiled at Rupert. He had a huge box in one hand, carefully balanced, but he extended the other for a hug.

I closed in carefully, trying not to upset the box, as I could smell something deliciously sugary and strawberry-ish coming from within it. I suspected that was my cake.

"Rupert, thanks for coming."

"Wouldn't miss this. I brought your birthday cake."

"I can smell it from here and it's making my mouth water."

"Miss Bethany made it for you. She's also here and already heading for the kitchen to help with making all those pizzas."

"Reinforcements," I said in relief. "Truly, I didn't expect this many people all at once. I mean, I stretched the party out over five hours so people had a chance to drop in, eat, and leave. Not drop in and just stay."

"The pizzas are encouraging them to linger."

"More like giving them food comas. Here, put that down over here. I left a space for the cake."

Rupert put it down with a sigh of relief. "So afraid I'd drop that thing all the way here, despite the packaging spells. Oh, before I forget, spare me an hour or two tonight after the party ends. I've found a good manager for your strawberry empire, I think. I want your take on the woman before I hire her."

A female manager? Yes, please! I always liked seeing more women in careers. "Sounds good to me. I'll make the time."

Ophelia appeared out of thin air and gave me a firm squeeze. "Happy birthday, Jamie. I do wish you'd let me get you some kind of present."

"I really don't need anything," I answered truthfully. Or even want many things, truth be told. That could be bought, anyway. To assuage her, I pointed toward the photo booth set up under the canopy nearby. "But take a picture with me before you go. I'm collecting pictures of all my friends and family here today. I want to make a photobook of them later."

"What a charming idea." Ophelia nodded approvingly. "Oh, we should try to get a family picture in with you. Everyone else should be here shortly. I'll make sure it happens."

"That'd be awesome." I didn't say it, but I wanted to make a copy and send it to my family as well. I'd told them about everyone, of course—they'd read the copies of mine and Henri's case file notes—but seeing people was a different thing altogether.

Blowing out candles on a cake wasn't a thing here and really, I only had a cake because Henri had spilled the beans that cakes were a thing in my culture. So we didn't do that but just cut it up and let people gorge themselves on strawberry deliciousness. The food coma reached Level 2 with no end in sight.

It was quite the crowd here now. We had at least thirty people, some in uniform, some not. Penny had managed to get here for about an hour but a case called her away again. Gerring was currently feeding bites to Niamh, both of them flirting and completely oblivious to the outside world. It was cute watching them.

My birthday party was a success. It made me unreasonably happy just watching everyone.

Was this where I'd expected to be when I hit thirty? I have to say, being stuck on another world was nowhere on my bucket list. Looking about now at these people that had so many pieces of my heart, I wouldn't trade them for anything. Especially not my Henri. Every trial, every bit of pain, that led me to this man—he was worth it all.

"Jamie!"

Shaken out of the thought, I turned and saw Regina headed for me, Khan a comfortable weight in her arms. (Seriously, though, did she ever let him walk? Every time I saw that cat he was being carried.)

She gave me a one-armed hug and then sank back to beam at me. "I've got two birthday presents for you."

Of course she did. She was a queen and thereby above the rules. "I really do not need anything."

"You'll like these presents. First present: I just heard from Egon this morning. The trial for Soto ended with the judge awarding him life in prison for the murder of Celto."

I punched a fist in the air in victory. "Good job, judge. Seriously, that was a win I didn't expect. I was only hoping for twenty years or something, considering what he did."

"The judge ruled heavier on punishment because Soto was perfectly willing to kill an innocent as well. Lady Blatt's survival didn't mitigate his intentions."

"True, that. Okay, I'll take that birthday present with thanks."

"I thought you would." Eyes twinkling, she turned and gestured to the man with her. "And this is Mr. Torres, your second present."

What...? I didn't get how this was a present. I doubted the queen had brought me a stripper. Henri would have opinions about that.

Mr. Torres reached out to shake hands with me, wearing a grin that looked like nothing but anticipation. He was a short guy, round in the tummy, dark hair balding on top. He looked like he enjoyed food very, very much and wasn't ashamed to admit it.

"A pleasure to meet you, Ms. Edwards. I understand you made all of the pizzas here? The smell alone is enticing. I can't wait to try one."

"You're welcome to do so," I encouraged. Still had no idea why this guy was here.

Regina explained with a distinct twinkle in her eye. "Mr. Torres is a restaurant aficionado who has developed six of the best restaurants in this city. Henri is a devoted fan of at least three I believe. If there is anyone I know who will try the pizzas and recognize money on the table, it will be him." She leaned in before confiding knowingly, "I know very well that you want pizza parlors to be widespread in this world. Here's your best chance."

I loved this woman. I seriously owed her for this. "You are my favorite."

Regina leaned back with a smirk. "I know."

I owed her Girls' Night and a huge slice of strawberry cake. For now, though, "Mr. Torres, come with me. This table here is full of the pre-made pizzas. I'm happy to give you the recipe if you like it. The fun part about pizza is that there's all sorts of things you can put on top and make it to your personal taste."

He followed me to the table, picked up one that was more of a fully loaded mix—bacon, hamburger, onion, tomato, bell peppers, and jackna, which is rather like a pineapple. Close to a pineapple anyway. Without any hesitation, he put a bite into his mouth.

And then moaned in pleasure.

Hook, line, and sinker—I had him.

Excuse the evil chuckle.

He swallowed and looked at me with the best puppy eyes I'd ever seen on a human face. "Ms. Edwards. Please do give me the recipe. It's so simple, just bread, sauce, cheese, meats, and fruit but—it's the sauce, isn't it? The sauce is what makes it so delicious."

"The sauce and the bread, actually. If the bread is too thick or chewy it ruins the overall taste. I'll give you the recipe but..." I leaned in. "How about a profit share for it and a guarantee that the first pizza parlor will be in downtown Kingston? My dream is to be able to just get off work and go for pizza without having to cook it myself."

He held out a hand and sealed the deal without hesitation. "Done. We'll talk terms after this."

What a beautiful, beautiful birthday this was turning out to be.

Pi-pi-pi-pizzzzaaaaaaaa.

Jamie, you did not just create yet another business.

I don't have to do anything but enjoy it this time.

Is there anything you won't do to get your favorite foods in this world?

Murder. That's about it.

At least she has a limit. That's news to me.

Jamie's Notes to Herself:

Ellie is my friend. My bosom buddy. My comrade. SHE MADE ME A DISHWASHER.

I also found a slang dictionary! Too bad it's about fifty years out of date....

In other news, I now have custody over Eddy and that's a weird feeling, being responsible for someone's well being. He now has the apartment next to mine so I can keep an eye on him.

List of things I need next time I call home:
-More Kindles. So many Kindles
-A cell phone (mostly so Henri and Ellie can take it apart and backwards engineer it)
-More music
-Designs of a crockpot (I would do illegal things for a crockpot)
-More Korean dramas
-A good explanation of why I adopted a little brother before running it by my family first. Oops?

Also, memo to me: "Out of the woods" is yet another phrase that doesn't translate. At all.

Days of the Week
Earth – Draiocht
Sunday – Gods Day
Monday – Gather Day
Tuesday – Brew Day
Wednesday – Bind Day
Thursday – Hex Day
Friday – Scribe Day
Saturday – Rest Day

Months
Earth – Draiocht
January – Old Moon
February – Snow Moon
March – Crow Moon
April – Seed Moon
May – Hare Moon
June – Rose Moon
July – Hay Moon
August – Corn Moon
September – Harvest Moon
October – Hunter's Moon
November – Frost Moon
December – Blue Moon

Werespecies: werehorses, wereowls, weremules, werefoxes, weredogs, werebadger, weremouse, werewolves, werebeavers, wereelephants, werebears, wereweasels, wererabbits, werelizard, weredragons(?)

Thanks for reading *This Potion is Da Bomb*! Jamie and the gang are just getting started with the Queen's Own, and there's more trouble to come! Check it out in *All in a Name*!

Looking for a mystery steampunk featuring a kickass female in a reverse Tomb Raider/Indiana Jones novel? Where she deals in putting the troublesome magical artifacts back where they came from? Try *Rise of the Catalyst*!

In the mood for a complete series? Have you read any of *The Human Familiar* series? It hits all the spots: unique magic, end-of-the-world baddies, and banter galore. Out of all my series, this is the most similar to *Case Files*! Check out *The Human Familiar*!

Who do you call when there's a curse? A sorcerer? A mage? A witch? What if all of those people have failed to remove it?

Well, call for an artifactor, of course.

Check out *The Child Prince*

Other books by Honor Raconteur
Published by Raconteur House
♫ Available in Audiobook! ♫

THE ADVENT MAGE CYCLE
Jaunten ♫
Magus ♫
Advent ♫
Balancer ♫

ADVENT MAGE NOVELS
Advent Mage Compendium
The Dragon's Mage ♫
The Lost Mage

WARLORDS (ADVENT MAGE)
Warlords Rising
Warlords Ascending
Warlords Reigning

ANCIENT MAGICKS
Rise of the Catalyst ♫

THE ARTIFACTOR SERIES
The Child Prince ♫
The Dreamer's Curse ♫
The Scofflaw Magician♫
The Canard Case♫
The Fae Artifactor ♫

THE CASE FILES OF HENRI DAVENFORTH
Magic and the Shinigami Detective♫
Charms and Death and Explosions (oh my)♫
Magic Outside the Box ♫
Breaking and Entering 101♫*
Three Charms for Murder
Grimoires and Where to Find Them
Death Over the Garden Wall
This Potion is Da Bomb
All in a Name
A Matter of Secrets and Spies

DEEPWOODS SAGA
Deepwoods ♪
Blackstone
Fallen Ward

Origins
Crossroads
Jioni

FAMILIAR AND THE MAGE
The Human Familiar
The Void Mage
Remnants
Echoes

GÆLDORCRÆFT FORCES
Call to Quarters

IMAGINEERS
Imagineer
Excantation

KINGMAKERS
Arrows of Change ♪
Arrows of Promise
Arrows of Revolution

KINGSLAYER
Kingslayer ♪
Sovran at War ♪

SINGLE TITLES
Special Forces 01
Midnight Quest

THE TOMES OF KALERIA
Tomes Apprentice ♪
First of Tomes ♪
Master of Tomes ♪

File X: Author

Honor Raconteur was born loving books. Her mother read her fairy tales and her father read her technical manuals, so was it any wonder she grew up thinking all books were wonderful? At five, she wrote and illustrated her first book.

At *mumbles age* she's lost count of how many books she's written and has no intention of stopping before she climbs into a grave. Right now, she lives in Michigan in a wonderful old Craftsman house with two dogs, three cats, and a fish.

For more information about her books, to be notified when books are released, or get behind the scenes info about upcoming books, sign up for her newsletter at honorraconteur.news@raconteurhouse.com

    www.honorraconteur.com
    FB: Honor Raconteur's Book Portal
    Patreon